MY FATHER'S
GARDENS

MY FATHER'S GARDENS

KAREN LEVY

HOMEBOUND
PUBLICATIONS
Independent Publisher of Contemplative Titles

For bulk ordering information or permissions write:
Homebound Publications, PO Box 1442
Pawcatuck, Connecticut 06379 United States of America

Title is also available in ebook editions.
VISIT OUR WEBSITE WWW.HOMEBOUNDPUBLICATIONS.COM

FIRST EDITION
ISBN: 978-1-938846-03-8 (pbk)

BOOK DESIGN

Cover Image Attributions:
© Asaf Eliason [Shutterhock.com]
© Turovsky [Shutterhock.com]
© vicspacewalker [Shutterhock.com]
© Jelena Veskovic [Shutterhock.com]
Photos at back of book provided by author © Karen Levy
Cover and Interior Design: Leslie M. Browning

Library of Congress Cataloging-in-Publication Data

Levy, Karen, 1966- author.
    My father's gardens / Karen Levy.
      pages cm
    ISBN 978-1-938846-03-8 (pbk.)
    1. Israelis—United States—Biography. 2. Jews—Israel—Biography. 3. Israel—Biography. 4. United States—Biography. I. Levy, Karen, 1966- II. Title.
    E184.37.L48M92 2013
    956.94'004924—dc23
    [B]
                                                                    2012048167

10 9 8 7 6 5 4 3 2 1

To Mark
for lighting the way home
and being there when I arrived.
And for Emma & Bailey
my finest creations.

Prologue: Leave-taking

Israel, 2006

This is the second time I have threatened to leave, swearing never to return. I had made this journey before but those other times, no one asked if I wanted to, and as a young child our coming and going seemed like an adventure. Decisions had been made, airline tickets purchased, my life arranged for me by others who believed they knew best. By the time I was twelve I had left Israel three times and could pack a suitcase in ten minutes flat. Unlike my best friend Ronit, who fretted over what she would salvage if her apartment ever caught fire, I used to lie in bed and picture the inside of my suitcase, the one with the big ugly flowers, unlike any that grew in my father's garden. I knew exactly what would fit in its compact rectangular space, how my books, journal, favorite stuffed animal and toiletries would fall into place as the zipper flew round on its dizzying course. A handful of stationery could easily fit into a side pocket, the opening lines of a letter to my dearest friend already started before the plane gathered itself into the air. Everything else in my room could stay. At some point we would be back.

It wasn't until I was older that I began to understand that there was more to our frequent exits and entries between Israel and America; More than an invitation for father to teach psychology for the summer or for a year at a university in California. But by then I had already caught the restlessness from which my mother suffered, seeing Israel through her overly critical eyes and not with the quiet love my father secretly felt for it. The first time Israel and my mother's impatience for it drove me away was at age twenty, standing on the last metal step in the predawn light, my back to the plane's mouth, my face towards the airport and all the bureaucracy spreading like vines behind it. I had spent the last two years in a green uniform, serving the country into which I was born, experiencing what most young Israelis do when they are fresh out of high school. The army taught me many lessons of which I was not to speak, and many others I am certain my mother wished I would soon forget. I now knew how to swear, shoot to maim, shower and dress in the dead of night, and keep secrets. I was now independent of my mother, not to the degree that I could thwart her openly, but just enough to learn that disobeying was an option. I had found a voice with which I loudly declared my farewell to this country, right before the plane was about to take me away once again to America, the place to which my family seemed to escape whenever my mother tired of this demanding land.

But of course the threats were empty and we returned; nostalgia mingled with guilt propelling my mother back to the land which refused to set us free. And since that day, I have taken off and landed between my two worlds more times than I care to count. Suspended in air, the shores of both lands always seem welcoming, the familiar flutter in my stomach at the sight of one, a sigh of relief as I arrive at the other. And somewhere in my luggage can be found a small bag containing the seeds of a garden I have slowly been transplanting and recreating on foreign soil.

Twenty years later I find myself making the same declaration, once again in an Israeli airport, and this time I think I mean it. I am finally answering the question I have battled with all these years. And while the few weeks visiting my father contributed to the decision I was about to make, it was the airport official sitting behind her glass cubicle who forced me to make up my mind, once and for all.

My Voice

What time is it, girl?" Two heads are peering down at me, one dark one light, giggling and nudging each other across the windowsill of their bedroom. I am standing in the courtyard below, watching bees working their way into the silky Hibiscus blossoms until they completely disappear, their velvety bodies swallowed in the sweet tunnels. Later, when we become friends, these girls will teach me how to pluck the flowers and suck the nectar, liquid gold on my tongue. But right now they are asking for the time. I look at the watch on my left wrist, a gift from my grandmother for the first day of school in this new but not new land. Red leather band, swiveling on my too narrow wrist; glass face with numbers I cannot read just yet. Even if I could I would not know how to say what the tiny metal hands are showing. Not on this side of the world where letters crawl across the page from right to left and two thirty in the afternoon is siesta time when children should not be outside disturbing the neighbors' rest.

While in America, father had been teaching me to read Hebrew every evening, the two of us perched on barstools at the kitchen counter, a plate of cookies and glasses of sweet American milk to wash down the thorny sounds of our language. In the house we spoke Hebrew, outside English; Mother's rule. This way, she reasoned, we would not forget our voices, would not abandon who we are. And here I stand, put to the test, my tongue unable to make the right sounds come out.

"Rega!" One minute! I yell out to the girls, my voice a croak

| 3

in my own ears, before I run into the house to ask my mother how to say what they expect to hear. But by the time I come back they are gone and I am alone again, watching bees. Years later the sisters admit that they had not really wanted to know the time. They just wanted to hear the new girl speak, curious to hear the sound of my voice. So was I.

*   *   *

A long and narrow piece of land covered in rough blades of grass wraps around our new house on 35 *Narkisim* Street. It offers nothing but lawn that leaves my legs dotted with small nicks and cuts, and a lone tree with heart shaped leaves the size of my palm. I don't know this yet, but come spring this unassuming tree will burst into the most amazing tulip shaped purple flowers. Their petals will feel satiny between my fingers when I collect them from the lavender carpet they create as they float to the ground. I am new here, sights and sounds introducing themselves like the neighbors who are peering at us from behind their shades, intrigued by anything that will break the monotony of daily life. Later in the season this tree will surprise me once more when its pods turn brown and brittle, bursting open in small crackling explosions, pelting me with round disc-like seeds I will collect in the folds of my shirt, my plan to create new trees. I must know that one day we will leave and part of the landscape will have to come with me.

Not all the neighbors are welcoming, though. Our villa as it is called is attached by one wall to the apartment building facing the street, six other families sharing the same address. The tenants on the third floor insist on parking their car in the narrow strip of asphalt under our windows, a show of force to put those Americans in their place; Funny how in Israel we are considered Americans, while in America we are just another family of immigrants. A second neighbor chains an old rowboat to our tree, an attempt to prove that the rectangle of grass behind our house belongs to them as well. Polite Europeans that they are, my parents are not well versed in revenge, an art I silently study as I watch Yoram, a neighbor's boyfriend, tie his Doberman to the boat, indignant on my parents' behalf. We soon regain use of our lawn once the vessel's owners realize they have been out-witted, their fear of the dog greater than the resentment they feel toward my family and our supposed wealth. Yet the Cohen family who lives on the first floor finds another way to flex their muscles, insisting that my father pull up the bean plants he had been tending in the modest vegetable garden, begun shortly after we moved in. Mr. Cohen claims that both his young daughters are allergic, angrily demanding my father destroy the plants at once. I can't understand how we have managed to upset so many people in the brief time since our arrival in this land to which my mother insists we belong.

* * *

"Make her say something."

Girls are twisted around in their seats, prodding each other, challenging one another to get me to speak so they can hear my accent. Their eyes do not seem to hold malice, just mischief, but I am mortified anyway, my first day of third grade in a new Israeli school terrifying enough. My new friend Ronit, comes to the rescue for the second time this morning, the first having taken place in the schoolyard below when my mother and I arrived. The green school uniform hung limply from her thin shoulders as her mother pushed her towards me recognizing the nervous-ness in my eyes. Ronit had taken me by the hand and led me to the assembly where we were soon swallowed in a sea of other green clad students before dispersing up the stairs to our respective classrooms in the enormous stone building.

"Leave her alone!" Ronit now hisses a command, already protective of me despite our very recent introductions, her familiarity with these girls obvious from the lack of fear in her voice. The classroom door swings open and in walks our teacher, a tall woman with thick glasses whose mission in the next few days will be to get me to smile. When I finally do she will call my mother to tell her. Chair legs scrape against the tile floor as the class rises to greet her in a chorus of young voices. "*Boker tov hamora!*" Good morning teacher! This respectful ritual is new to me and I follow suit, relieved when my accented Hebrew is swallowed in the loud crowd whose voices and gestures I will grow to love over the next three years I am allowed to spend in their midst.

Wings

Within my mother's reach I am good. Under her roof I can do no wrong as long as I follow her rules. In her courtyard my wings shudder at the sight of so much sky, but the buildings have too many prying eyes and my wings stay folded, out of sight. Out of the courtyard, past blood red Hibiscus and the watchful old kleptomaniac on the first floor of 37 *Narkisim*, the street beckons and my wings awkwardly flutter loose. In a few years they will learn to unfurl much faster, gathering force on my way down the stairs from my room, bursting out the heavy front door, exploding into flight, the crimson of the Hibiscus a velvety blur. Where will I fly? Down our street, across the boulevard, father's footsteps a distant obligatory tattoo, soon lost. Am I too fast, or does he know, how good it feels to run as if your life depended on it? I will learn to fly, across the train tracks, into waiting arms and sky blue eyes in which I drown. Until then I am good, in my sensible clothes, my tight braids, two hours of piano practice every afternoon, Chopin waltzes escaping through the open window as the sound of neighborhood kids drifts in, more enchanting than my melodies. I am well-behaved, predictable. A hothouse flower trained to bloom out of season and in the wrong climate. I do not belong.

I Want

Israel, 1975

Throughout my life I will envy people. In fourth grade I secretly long for the small cloth pencil holder the next-door neighbor, Tali produces one afternoon, sprawled on the grass beneath my mother's windows. She unzips it confidently with one sharp tug of nail polished fingers and sun bronzed hand, and from inside she fishes hard colorful candy, sweet marbles, the kind most common at the corner kiosk and on which I will never spend my allowance. "A waste of money," mother says. "Save it." For what, I'm not sure, since what I need is bought for me, and what I want requires my mother's approval. Expressing desire implies a lack and my mother, forever determined to prove herself as a perfect parent, is adamant that we lack for nothing.

Tali's candy is smooth on my tongue, hard against my teeth, leaving tiny bumps in my left cheek where I will treasure its sweetness, until it melts into nothing but a warm memory. The pantry in my mother's kitchen is filled with Viennese chocolates my grandfather sends and I'm always allowed to have. But I'm drawn to the local *Petel*, colorful sugar candy sold in clear plastic bags at the corner kiosk, the kind the neighborhood kids pull out of their pockets, dipping their fingers, staining them brilliant sunset oranges and reds. Unlike Tali's, my pencil holder has nothing but neatly sharpened pencils, an eraser and the smell of the classroom. Like me it contains no secrets, yet.

Secrets

Beautiful families keep ugly secrets, contained in pretty boxes. Our box is extra-large with fancy ribbons, and every one of my friends wants to be me. They want to travel to America, miss the first day of school when they return, sleep on double mattresses in a room filled with American toys and souvenirs from faraway places. But there are days when I want to come from the ugly families, the ones whose secrets spill out windows and hurtle through doors followed by high pitched shrieking and a well-aimed shoe. In the apartment building across the way, the woman on the top floor is angry at the world, but takes it out on her young daughter. Every so often it rains toys, clothes, childhood possessions this frustrated mother sends soaring like unsuccessful exorcisms. All of us know her misery, and no one is surprised when years later, the daughter turns hooker and the mother accidentally sets fire to herself and goes up in flames, this time ensuring that the demons will not return. For weeks I imagine her charred body in my mind's eye, seeing her in the darkness of my room as I struggle for sleep.

Two floors down another act unfolds in our neighborhood's daily theater. From these lower windows different sounds announce themselves. Sisters are fighting over clothing in one room, while in the kitchen I watch their mother filling up the space around her with her bulk and her bitterness, frying up the fish her husband caught on his way home from the factory. She complains that he spends hours hip deep in water, bringing home endless proof of his whereabouts, filling her clean kitchen with shiny fish scales she resents. But we all know that his afternoons are spent in the arms of a Russian woman who must not mind his habits or his fish. *She must be a mermaid,* I imagine but keep to myself, since I'm just a kid and not really supposed to know. I collect these whispered confessions, bits of gossip handed out with the change at the small kiosk down the street where I'm sent to buy milk. Those women I watch with grocery nets slung over their arms see me coming and stop their chatter; exchanging knowing looks that make me think I may have been the topic of conversation. All I catch is "...the professor's daughter..."and the rest they save for their afternoon tea. Our ugliness is kept from me and, so my mother believes, from everyone else, not like those other people's lives, swirling about, drifting through windows uninvited like the yellow dust the sand storms bring in summer. It will be years before I discover that my father has been visiting mermaids too.

*   *   *

I am not supposed to know this either, but my friend Orna told me that she overheard her mother on the phone talking about our classmate Nirit being adopted. Her mother warned her not to say anything, but Orna decided to tell me because, she casually declares, I look like someone who can keep secrets. That evening I study my face in the mirror above my dresser, trying to figure out what Orna could have meant and what it is about my face that made her think I could be trusted. Looking back at me is a pair of dark brown eyes, "chocolate almonds" my mother always says. A face I think is too round and thick eyebrows I will grow to resent. No mischief or naughtiness lurks anywhere in my features, and the seriousness of my stare startles me a bit. I sit on the edge of my bed wishing Orna hadn't told me what she overheard, since I don't know whether the secret is one Nirit wishes to keep to herself or one of which she is a part, unaware of her true origins as well. And now that I think of it, her parents seem awfully old, quiet and shuffling about the house across the street where I've only visited a handful of times. I wonder what it must be like knowing that you'd been given up by the people who should want you most, and whether it would be better not to know at all. I decide never to breathe a word of this new information entrusted to me, but I never look at Nirit the same way again, part of me feeling sorry for her loss. The other part wishes I were adopted too. Perhaps less would be expected of me if there were fewer people to live up to.

*　*　*

Not that there are that many people left in our family. My mother is adamant about reminding me that we have few relatives left because of the horrors that befell so many at the hands of the Nazis. She usually brings up the subject if I have been unkind about members of our reduced tribe, whether I complain about a nagging aunt or display impatience with my younger brother. A somber expression takes over her face and out come the stories, bits and pieces of history to make me understand why it is so important that we stay united. She reminds me about my grandfather's twin brother, Freddie, who was taken to Auschwitz where he later perished. She speaks of her parents' narrow escape from German officials using false documents and impeccable German. Her tales describe suitcases packed with the pretense of a summer outing, family heirlooms left behind in what my mother describes as a lavish Warsaw apartment, never to be seen again. The way she describes the contents of these lost rooms makes me think that she would rather be back there again, eating at the claw footed dining room table, heated by the fancy tiled stove, while the help saw to the cooking and cleaning. Astounded, I listen as she reveals that she was not told she was Jewish until the age of thirteen, an attempt to protect her during dangerous times. Her eyes glisten as she recalls the mystery of Christmas Eve, when the tall double doors of the living room would be closed while a beautiful pine tree was being decorated. Her Catholic upbringing is woven into the tapestry of my childhood stories, remnants of her wartime past surfacing when she allows my brother and me to leave milk and cookies for Santa Claus whenever we find ourselves in America on Christmas Eve. Everything seems to have been better back then, a past filled with chivalrous men, ladylike women, and children who knew their place.

We are missing family members I will never get to meet, left only with vague stories from which too many details are missing. I am told about my Hungarian paternal grandfather, captured and later released only to die from an illness before he could reach his home. My father, in a rare moment of revelation, tells me that all he recalls of his own father is a shadowy figure leaning over his bed when he was two years old. I hear brief descriptions of my maternal great grandmother who stubbornly refused to leave her home, sending her two daughters to safety and never heard from again. These people are wraith like figures in my history, their images captured in fading photographs with scribbled names and dates on the pictures' curling backs. They are offered up to me as parts of my inheritance, like an old unwieldy mantle I want to shrug off. I would much rather rewrite myself, searching the books on my shelves for just the right character to be.

Instead of reverence and respect I begin to resent these ghosts whose deaths seem to dictate my behavior. I am not only expected to be more tolerant of the living, but entire days are dedicated to the dead. Memorial days, remembrance days, ceremonies at school for which we are told to show up in white shirts, the girls in skirts, in place of our green uniforms, to sit through lengthy poetry readings. On *Yom Hashoah*, Holocaust Remembrance day, places of public entertainment are closed by law; the television airs nothing but war documentaries, while the radio plays mournful tunes. And at ten a.m., no matter where you might be, sirens sound throughout Israel for two whole minutes. Cars stop in the middle of highways, drivers exit, their doors left yawning open, and people stand frozen in their places in silent tribute to the dead. In the presence of death everyone knows how to behave. Yet despite the solidarity this one day seems to engender, I feel only a vague connection to it all, the rituals more a chore than a connection that unites.

Perhaps I am not convinced by these annual displays of sadness and restraint because people appear to forget what unites us the rest of the year. On days when the memories of the dead are not hovering as close, mothers screech at children, teenagers mouth off to parents, and teachers punish students. Bus drivers slow to their stops a few meters past their stations, just enough to make waiting passengers run to catch up. Those very same drivers who so readily stopped right there in their tracks, now cut each other off, car lights flashing, horns blaring in frustration over the slightest delay. Unlike Americans who smile at each other whether acquainted or not, Israelis walk down streets with their eyes on their destination, no acknowledging nods at unknown passersby, always ready to do battle.

We are less tolerant of each other despite the terrible history we still see tattooed on bare arms of relatives. Quick to anger despite the ever-present threat of neighboring Arab countries against whom our borders are heavily guarded. Perhaps years of persecution and daily terrorism were having the opposite effect

I thought they should. Instead of bringing us closer they were sending people away, to places like America where some of my friends believed I did nothing other than visit Disney Land and rub shoulders with movie stars; America, where anyone could become anything they ever dreamed they could be. More and more Israelis were heading out and away, while my mother dug deeper into the past, hanging on to its ghosts as if letting go would erase her from this earth.

Dirty Laundry

Israel, Any Given Afternoon

The neighbor in the building to our left begins her arguments inside the apartment and pours them out the kitchen window with the dirty water. On any given afternoon, I listen to the drama of her cheating husband being scolded in tones that rise higher as she cleans the sill beneath her window. She scrubs with ferociousness only I see, sweat gathering on her forehead as she pours her misery into the sill. An Israeli Lady Macbeth, cleaning away the ugliness her husband, the sergeant major brings home with his sweat stained uniforms. An occasional demand for "Sheket!", "Quiet!" comes from a neighboring window, not because they don't want to know, but because we've already heard it. My mother would never allow the neighbors to know what she really thinks of my father. We aren't like other families, bringing their problems to my father's study where the respected psychologist fixes them and sends them on their way. We have no problems, my mother believes, while all through our neighborhood people's indiscretions and troubles are discussed like the latest Friday night Arab drama on television. Even their laundry hangs in plain view, stretched on lines pulled under windows, dripping on parked cars below. Empty green uniforms, like so many lifeless soldiers, swaying in the breeze; Undergarments in all shapes and sizes brazenly flapping for all to see. From our lines, hidden behind a concrete wall, hang bath towels dried stiff from the sun, scorched and scratchy against my face as I breathe in their summery scent. No one will ever see what we really wear under our proper American bought clothes. On the outside we make a good impression. We live in the big *villa* attached only by one wall to the apartments facing our street while everyone else I know lives in small flats. But come inside and see that our walls are damp in winter, and the narrow heater hanging in the bathroom doesn't warm me, no matter how many times mother tells me to lift my face to it and pretend it's the sun. When thunderstorm season arrives, the electricity simply gives up, and the stairwell turns into a gallery of shadows thrown onto the walls in disturbing forms. "There's nothing to be afraid of," my mother repeats, and I'd like to believe her, but I can't. I'd like to keep thinking that we're special, different; immune. But there's a voice inside that warns me, *something bad is coming.* Father is three floors down, sitting behind a heavy wooden desk, teaching his patients how to master their fears, while his wife is upstairs, reminding her daughter what good stock she's from. And the disappointment they feel in each other is an entity filling the house with unspoken regret. *Why is he always buried in a book,* her eyes accuse, watching him. *Why isn't she ever satisfied,* his sighs whisper, while he keeps silent.

Yet our good name always saves us and sets us apart. One mention of my father's name, and my teachers treat me with respect other students are rarely granted. One foot in the door of the medical clinic where my maternal grandmother works and I am kindly shown in no matter how many patients sit suffering in the waiting room. And our behavior must distinguish us as well. We don't call to each other from window to window like the local gossips with the latest piece of news. *We* don't show public displays of affection like that *freha,* cheap woman sitting on her boyfriend's lap in *public.* Just once, I'd like to be like everyone else. Bumped and bruised by the real world out there, the one I know is waiting for me in those dark shadows.

The Doctor is In

Israel, Father's Study

My father, the psychologist, does not speak much about his work. And as a timid child I do not ask too many questions. Later, on one of our many forays to the United States, he will thrill me by inviting me to attend a university lecture and I will sit, filled with pride, listening to the man to whose silence I had become accustomed eloquently explain the finer points of social psychology to semi-interested freshmen. I will be no less impressed by the admiring group of female students fawning over him at the lecture's end.

Yet on occasion, my father's work is sitting in the makeshift waiting room in the entrance of our house on *Narkisim* Street, distractedly thumbing through magazines as we all pretend not to see each other while I make my way up the stairs to my mother. Whatever difficulties his clients have brought for the good doctor to solve remain cloaked in mystery on the first floor, in the hushed study where they sit across the heavy wooden slab of a desk my mother discovered in a cramped antique shop by the port of Haifa. The study smells of old books and worn leather, the shelves laden with volumes in English, Hebrew, German, Hungarian and French, my father challenging himself to read texts in their original language, forever adding information to the wealth of knowledge he already possesses. I wander into his room when he's away, allowing myself to briefly sit on the worn leather chair behind the massive desk, seeing the world from my father's view, imagining what it would be like to have so many strangers depend on me to fix them so they might be happy again.

Sometimes though, my father's work walks timidly up the stairs to use the bathroom on the second floor, smiling shyly if I happen to be in the living room watching. She surprises me whenever I find her standing there on the landing, and I think she must have tiptoed all the way up without so much as a rustling of her lengthy skirt for me not to have noticed. Her dull brown hair hangs loosely around her wide face, broad shoulders slightly stooped in spite of her young years as if trying to hide her heaviness from the world. And when she leaves, a faint scent of patchouli floats in her wake; its sweet and musky smell lingering on the stairs long after she has retreated to the safety of her own home. When I ask my father who she is, all he can say about his client is that she has trouble leaving her house, venturing out less and less until even the dentist has to come to her. On her birthday my father buys a bouquet of flowers he asks me to deliver to her home a few blocks away. I set out on my task, wondering what could be so frightening between here and there, and what could possibly have happened to keep her from enjoying the sense of belonging that the simple act of walking down familiar streets gives me and which I so long for when I am away.

There is one other occasion when my father's work spills into our world yet in a more aggressive way the night the doorbell rings and I go downstairs to answer it. The large man in the entrance asks if the doctor is in, and before I have a chance to stop him, he pushes past me and bursts into the study where my father is in session with what turns out to be the man's wife. I stand transfixed by the angry yelling of the accusing husband, the wife's plaintive attempts to defend herself, my father's raised voice instructing her to go upstairs until her husband can be calmed. By now I have inched my way to the study door where I glimpse the almost comical sight of my thin-framed father, his forearm stretched across the broad chest of the jealous husband, pinning him against the wall as the woman runs past me on her way up to the safety of the second floor. She leaves soon after, her husband staying behind until peace is restored to the generally calming atmosphere of the study where even the noise of traffic from the main road is muted, thick walls and the room's almost subterranean location compared to the rest of the house, creating another world. These brief glimpses into other people's lives, their fears and doubts seeping out of my father's study where they are usually contained and controlled, make me realize that our family too can be touched by the frailties of human nature, as fallible as any other.

Lessons

My mother's lessons are taught in bits and pieces, memory fragments I collect over years of watching her do battle with the world. She demonstrates how to walk into a room as though I own it, as if preparing to be thrown out of places in which she must fear we do not belong. Does she know I'd rather fold into myself and disappear? She shows me how to hold my head up and stare people down before they have a chance to get the better of me. *I didn't know they wanted to,* I tell myself inside. In her lighthearted moments she sashays across the room, teaching me to swing my hips before I've figured out what good they're for. Later, when I discover the hidden powers nature has bestowed, mother never allows me out of her sight long enough to use them. She has managed to combine her stiff European upbringing with the vulgar behavior Israelis display just to survive. By the time I graduate from my mother's academy with a mixture of primness and bluntness, I can elbow my way on to a bus, give my seat up for an elderly passenger like I was taught, stare down a line jumper at the local post office, politely thank the clerk for the stamps, perform Chopin nocturnes at the local music conservatory dressed in my finest, then sleep with the violinist. I'm like those grafted trees proud gardeners show off, the fruit half plum, half peach or some other such strange anomaly.

But the day I graduate from my mother's finishing school will also be the day I fall from grace, my mother's good grace that is. In the meanwhile I follow the mental etiquette book that is her guide. Both hands must be in view on the dining table. Fork on the left, knife on the right, sharp edge facing in, eat with the left, cut with the right, *always*. (Invited to dinner during one of our stays in the United States, my mother watches in horror as our American hosts cut their food, lay down their knives, reach for their forks with their *right* hand while their left rests in their laps, *under* the table. She later inquires of me whether I knew what they did under there. I did not.) Hands are never stuffed into pockets, arms never folded across chest. Shuffling of feet is a sign of laziness, change jingled in pockets, arrogance. Never ask for anything, say thank you whether you like the present or not; and above all, no disobeying of mothers.

So many lessons passed down; And for what? None of this training works when the landscape changes. When desert becomes snowy peaked mountains, and warm Mediterranean turns into dramatic Pacific Ocean cliffs, when loud-mouthed Israelis are replaced by mild-mannered Protestants, all the rules of engagement change. I have to learn which self to wear; how loud and pushy, subdued or meek I should be, depending on the landscape and the proximity of my mother.

Shoes

Israel, 1976

I know winter has arrived when the ugly suede shoes appear. They stare at me from across the room where mother has prepared them for the following day along with my freshly laundered school uniform. I'm not particular about my clothes. Not like the sisters in the apartment across the courtyard, squabbling endlessly; their voices rising precariously when one has dared to disturb the razor sharp pleats of the other's pants. They keep these treasured items folded neatly on soap-scented shelves, the arrangement a fashion statement in itself and just as telling about their natures. I suppose the importance I lend to shoes says something about me, as well. What, I don't know just yet. But shoe shopping days are trying times for my mother, who isn't interested in how they look but whether they are made well enough to support my feet, and last. All I know is that I love the sound of the wooden clogs some of my friends wear, the clip clop such a carefree, festive sound, like small hooves on pavement. And the leather sandals all the cool girls wear, their big toe looped through its own ring, their sweaty toe imprints left behind in the well-worn leather even after they've taken them off. "I don't know how they can stand that thing between their toes," my mother marvels. She relents and presents me with a pair of lemon yellow clogs, tiny air holes scattered across their domed tops like so many freckles. But each time I wear them my mother frets about the terrible effects they will have on my ankles, my future aches and pains guaranteed by the support these silly shoes fail to provide. And when I wear them to school one day, a teacher comes to the door of the classroom I had just passed, calling after me to be lady like and walk more quietly. I don't look back but I do make my steps a bit heavier as I stomp down the rest of the hallway, his eyes boring into my back.

Our shoe purchasing takes place only in the finest of shops, where my mother warns the salesman about my narrow feet, "all the women in our family share this trait," the tendency of my arches to fall, no indication of weakness here, just further evidence of our good breeding. With no sign of being impressed, the clerk measures my right foot, trapping it in the silver metal contraption that tells him all he needs to know, a fortune-teller of sorts reading my feet. My mother informs him that my left foot is slightly longer, a fact I wish she'd keep to herself despite her assurances that everyone's feet share this discrepancy. She also declares that truly beautiful women always have one eye slightly smaller than the other, a claim that sends me to the mirror unsure of which I'd rather be, truly beautiful or not, considering the strangeness of this assertion.

I watch the salesman's back as he climbs the rolling ladder, expertly maneuvering across the honeycombed face of the dim wall, where boxes of shoes are stacked from floor to ceiling in identical rows he seems to read, like a blind man running his fingers across a book of Braille. Having plucked a box out of its cubby, he rolls back towards us down the narrow passage between shoes and counter, jumping off the ladder and completing his circus act. I'm imagining the wondrous pair of shoes the box in his hand must contain. The shimmer of sequins, the loveliness of a small heel, the shapeliness of leather straps encircling my ankles. The possibilities are endless, heroines of films and novels parading past me in surefooted glamour. Instead, there between the brown papers in which they are wrapped are the ugly suede shoes, their toes squared off; their laces promising to keep my ankles from straying. It is as if my mother believes the sturdiness of my shoes will ensure the sensible path I will follow. But I don't want sensible shoes. I want excitement only a stiletto can promise, forget what it might do to my arches. I want confidence only a velvety boot can send up my well-behaved spine. I'd even settle for the cuteness a leathery, beaded moccasin would bestow as I softly padded down the hushed aisles of a classroom during an exam.

My mother's concern for the well-being of my feet prevails. We walk out of the shop with the suede shoes lodged safely in their box, and the salesman's guarantee that they will last me the entire season, perhaps even the next. "You need good shoes for school, you're not going to a fashion show," my mother defends herself against the disappointment on my face. And there is no point arguing, I'd only sound ungrateful. Just like that time when the folklore instructor said we needed black shoes for class, and my heart had leapt at the thought of what my feet could do encased in the feisty splendor of a Flamenco pump. Mother had searched her closet and found a leathery pair of shoes with ugly heels, the kind old women in sagging nylons wore to market. "Why go out and buy shoes when we've got perfectly good ones right here?" I had clomped my way across the dance floor, visions of golden skinned men asking me to dance evaporating each time I glimpsed my feet in the large mirror on the opposite wall.

One day, I promise myself as I give the laces an angry yank before I head out the door to school. *One day,* I'll fill my closet shelves with glorious shoes that will help me get anywhere I want to go.

My Name

My name makes little sense in Israel and less so in America, where even its spelling, Karen, misleads people to incorrect pronunciations. "Caren," I repeat without fail after every introduction, people leaning forward, watching my mouth like lip readers trying to capture the sound I make as I caw out my name. "Caaa ren," I repeat as they smile politely and nod no closer to understanding. And although in Hebrew my name doesn't make people feel like their mouths are filled with rocks, my third grade teacher still suggests my mother change it to something more Israeli, adding herself to the list of individuals my mother dislikes. I listen to other children's names as they are read in class on the first day of school, tasting them on my tongue like newly offered sweets. Israeli names I translate as they bloom into their definition around me, *Vered*, pretty as the rose her name describes, *Iris*, lean and lovely. *Dalia*, bright and showy as she raises her hand in response to the teacher's calling of her name. I *should have been a Violet*, I think to myself as I shrink into my seat, waiting for my turn to explain, to repeat, to wish away a name that has no explanation in a world where I need to make sense.

In America my envy of others' names grows worse, the field from which my parents could have picked dizzying in its possibilities. *Pearl* shimmers in the seat across the classroom aisle from me, while *Grace* drapes herself over the arm of a boy she likes. *Dorothy* lays claim to the Emerald City, while *Elizabeth* gets to be regal or just plain *Lizzy* when it suits her. Like titles of books in which I search for someone who will tell me how to be me, these names contain the blueprints of their owners, glimpses of potential lives they may one day lead. If only I could have been an *Esperanza* filled with hope to carry me through uncertain times. Or *Joy*, promising happiness to those I meet.

Even a *Wendy* would do, dreaming at the window until Peter came to whisk me away to his Never Land. My mother should have listened to the Israeli hospital clerk who argued and refused to accept the name she offered on the forms the day I was born. Perhaps he had seen what she could not when he looked down into the crib where I lay waiting for my story to begin.

Fear

ear is not an option in our house. Any display of timidity
is a sign of weakness. This training begins early, long before I come along and provide the clay my mother molds.
Over the years, my father has learned to suppress emotions in
my mother's presence, although I see sadness in his eyes from
time to time when he sits lost in thought, in the very same room
yet far from where we are, a book cradled in his lap. Away from
her disapproving eyes he is as silly as can be, his lack of concern
for others' opinions refreshing. On an outing to the grocery store
one afternoon, just the two of us, he suggests racing our shopping cart down the produce aisle, the cart slipping away from us
and careening into the fruit bins while we both pick ourselves up
from the floor, laughing until tears come and earning the scorn-
ful looks of local housewives.

From her own mother mine has learned a strange defiance,
a need to prove strength built on false bravado. My grandmother, the beautiful woman I see in fading black and white photographs, twice married and always in charge, is still a tough act
to follow. And follow her, my mother does, loyal and unques-
tioning and filled with resentment I can almost touch but never
hear. It isn't until years later that my father reveals the extent of
the loyalty to which his wife willingly submitted. Newly married and pregnant, my mother aborted her first child because my
grandmother did not believe it was the right time. She took care
of the details, my father merely told not to worry. He had no
say in what would have been his first child, not then, a lifetime

before he discovers he has a voice and how good it feels to make it heard.

Yet by then we've all been trained in the uselessness of questioning the women in our family. When the sirens wail, signaling the beginning of the Yom Kippur war, we join the other tenants in the bomb shelter under the building. Within minutes my mother has had enough. Babies are crying, people are smoking, and floors are dirty; all unfit for the likes of us. Back upstairs we go, no matter that the all clear hasn't sounded yet. I'm taught that there is nothing to fear. Those bombs don't carry our names on their backs. We are untouchable. By the time the all clear sends its mournful lament into the skies, we have been busy at our tasks, unlike the other tenants whose footsteps we now hear in the stairwell as they trudge back up to their apartments.

My mother treats the elements much like she does war, as nothing to be feared. When the wind howls on a stormy night, she takes me out in the dark, sits me on her knee and with the breeze in my face, proves how foolish I am to be afraid of nature. She never denies that danger exists, but finds it crucial to prove she has the upper hand. My mother convinces me that our home is safe, but teaches that lights must be turned off were an intruder to ever break in; that way, she explains, I can see but not be seen. Rather than filling me with confidence, this bit of information causes me to lie awake at night staring into the thick darkness, listening intently for the tread of strangers on our stairs. When I fall, and I do so often, no mollycoddling is allowed. Despite my pleas, the injured limb is firmly forced into the tub, washed, then medicated, "You don't want it to get infected, do you?" And I'm told that my pain will pass by my wedding day. (Considering my young age, this promises an eternity of anguish.) At age seven, on the eve of the Yom Kippur war, I skin my knee and one glance is all that my mother needs to determine that infection is on its way. *Babcia*, my grandmother the surgeon is summoned, syringe for my Tetanus shot in hand, (she also just so happens to bring military boots my father had forgotten at her apartment and thus is jokingly accused by my mother for having started the war), and though I put up a good struggle, my small frame pushing against the laundry room door where I've barricaded myself, my grandmother's silhouette through the frosted window is stronger. I am saved from bacteria, when all I wanted was for father to come to my rescue. Yet ours is a family of strong women, and he is merely a downtrodden king, his silence his consent. My rescuing will have to be done by someone else.

Despite my mother's intolerance for cowardice, fear is a powerful teacher, and one of her favorite tools to get us to do what she wants. It moves in and makes itself comfortable, an unwanted guest overstaying a welcome never granted. Regardless of my mother's efforts to tell me it didn't exist, I know now that it arrived, years after it had already left. Years after it had pushed out love, because fear was stronger than love in my mother's household. Each one of her lessons was her way of fighting her own demons and introducing them to me. Now I know better. I grew up and realized there really wasn't a monster under the bed and my mother couldn't bring my world to a fiery end. Not when she herself was plagued by so many weaknesses. I've seen her on planes as the engines begin to rumble, reaching inside her blouse for the small golden medallion hidden there. No *Magen David*, protector of David hangs from this chain. And when I ask to see, my mother sheepishly shows me the delicate Madonna suspended between her Jewish breasts. War-time secrets no one talks about. My mother is protected by this Catholic talisman while she teaches me how to destroy my Israeli passport if our plane is ever hijacked. Girls who are taught to shred identification papers can't be afraid of walking up shadowy stairwells. So I keep my fears to myself and begin my search for someone who will protect me.

Potatoes

W alking home from school on any given day is a feast for my senses. It is time for the midday meal, a habit we will have to change when we arrive in America, where lunch is a hurried affair of sandwiches and potato chips. In the Israel of my childhood, shop owners lock their doors, children hurry home, and housewives bustle in narrow kitchens where they have busied themselves all morning. Out of windows float the warm smells of their creations; simmering stews, lids dancing above bubbling steam. Ronit's mother will be serving *burekas*, flaky phyllo dough stuffed with cheese and spinach and sprinkled with sesame seeds. By the time Ronit climbs the three flights of stairs to her apartment these savory triangles will be ready, steaming and fragrant and filled with her mother's Sephardic version of love. A few steps further, on the first floor of the next building, from behind Sara's shutters escape the scents of spices, rich satiny fragrances that make my surroundings familiar and warm. Today I smell frying onions and sweet paprika as I round the corner into our courtyard, and I know she must be making *chulent*, a meat and bean dish, thick enough for a spoon to stand. Sometimes I spend the afternoon in Sara's kitchen until my mother returns from work. I watch her large form, thick and ponderous become graceful as she prepares a typical Israeli salad, slicing tomatoes, cucumbers and peppers into tiny perfect squares, the sharp blade never missing a beat, the bowl before her filling with this colorful mosaic. Funny I think to myself, how such a large woman, her stubby fingers and painfully short nails so used to hard work, can create something so delicate and pretty for daughters whose bickering will cause her anger to surface before the meal is over.

Tonight, *Babcia* is coming to dinner, and with her will be Janek, her second husband and not really my grandfather, but I adore him nonetheless. I never tire of the memory he fondly recounts, of an evening when I was left in his care, requesting he read me story after story despite the late hour and the long gone bedtime. "Janek, Seepool!" I demanded, my three year old tongue incapable of pronouncing the "r" for the Hebrew word *seepoor,* story. My mother returned from her outing only to find me still gazing at the pile of children's books while Janek was seated on the floor beside me, propped against a wall, snoring his exhaustion. During the school year, he gladly arrives every time my teacher assigns a poster, and sits for hours beside me at the dining room table where he helps me draw and design, as if his training as an architect had been for this purpose all along. When school begins and it is time to wrap books in their protective coverings, Janek is the one who measures and cuts the thick waxy paper, his precise folds a work of art. And because he is at the table with us tonight, potatoes will be part of the meal, *kartofle* as he calls them in Polish, generously salting then spearing them on his fork. I once asked why he had to eat potatoes every day, and my mother explained that it was one of the few foods available when he was hiding in the forests during the war. He had made a pact with a fellow Partisan she said, promising that if they survived, they would eat potatoes with their dinners, every day for the rest of their lives. I watch in awe as he methodically chews each mouthful with a calm determination, and I don't even laugh when his jaw makes a repeated clicking sound with each bite he takes, the image of this man I admire, hungry in the cold woods too disturbing to make fun. As usual, a cold bottle of the dark malt beer he enjoys sits to the right of his plate, its brown glass glinting as he pours himself a small cup, wiping the frothy foam from his lips with the *shmate*, as my grandmother calls it, an old kitchen towel he keeps tucked into his shirt as he eats. He is oblivious to my grandmother's persistence that I eat more, to my mother's obsession with proper table etiquette, to the half dozen other dishes from which he may choose, *pierogi, borscht, compote, herring,* as he focuses on the plate before him.

And through our open window come the sounds of clinking dishes from neighboring apartments; smells of other meals mingling in the late afternoon air, swirling over tables where lives are shared, traditions continued, and promises to friends kept.

Howling

Israel, 1977

They said his mother had died in a car accident, and maybe that is why every once in a while, our young neighbor raises his voice to the skies beyond his bedroom ceiling and howls. The sound is annoying to my mother and she demands that my father *do* something, but I think his animal cries are terribly sad and lonely. If I stand on tiptoe at our kitchen window, I can just make out his swaying form between the iron safety bars that my mother insisted we have installed. I see a young man his eyes shut tight, a guitar clasped and accompanying these nightly symphonies. In the recesses of his apartment a phone rings, probably my father obeying his wife's complaints about the disturbance. The young man's father, apologetic, promises to end his son's cries, and for a short time peace is restored and sleep resumed; until again, the pain wells up and spills out into the night. Once more at the window, I see the father, face haggard from lack of wife and sleep, hanging gray laundry on the line beneath his window. He never looks up at me as he silently hangs the dripping clothes, his upper torso dressed in nothing but a sleeveless undershirt. And why should he speak? His son is saying enough for both of them. Their pain rolls out unchecked, and I wonder what would happen if I raised my face to the night skies and joined in. Mother would send father to silence me, too. Nice girls from good families have nothing to complain about.

Pitango

In the house behind the pitango tree lives a dark princess. I sit in her sparsely decorated room, watching in awe as she braids her long brown hair, my very own olive skinned Repunzel. Her strong brown fingers fly down her dark mane, taming it as I sit in silence, mesmerized by her skill. We are classmates, yet we rarely speak, my shyness only allowing me to admire Shlomit's easy ways from afar. But today I have dared to walk down the street and knock on her door. Her fingers reach the end of her thick, long braid and confidently flip it over her shoulder as she turns to watch me, curiously taking in my lady-like presence in her modestly furnished room. My Americanized bedroom with its ruffled white bedspread and matching curtains would never hold her as hers captivates me with its warm simplicity. No lace, no frills, no dresses which she refuses to wear until years later, when I see but don't recognize her in one. Everything about her is clean and precise, from her tiny handwriting in which she writes me a note, each letter sculpted and swirling into the next, to her chiseled face, smooth and tan and good to look at. I want to be her with all my being, and for awhile I try to imitate the guttural sound she makes when she speaks, a rasping at the roof of her mouth which a *Sabra* like me, native born, should be able to make. But I have been taught my sounds on different shores, and this throaty honesty she so easily produces would clash with my dresses and shock the good breeding out of mother. I never visit her again, but I keep a few pitango pits for future planting and her note, the one in which she wishes me a safe voyage to America and her hopes for my swift return.

Music

Israeli Sounds

Our neighborhood sings throughout the day, beginning with the clearing of throats that is the screeching of buses on the road between the port city of Haifa and the old crusade town, Acco. Red and white buses reluctantly pull up to their stations, their doors yawning open and whooshing shut with an angry snap. In buildings all around, shutters raised by pulleys are tugged upwards, like so many bleary eyes letting in the light of day. Soon car engines will cough to life, leaving the neighborhood to the cleaning women and housewives. Windows are thrown open and over railings hang bedding and rugs, apartments turned inside out for the world to see. Arab music spills out balconies as cleaning women beat rugs and wash the stone-tiled stairwells our feet will soon sully again. From my window I can see the alley where peddlers cry their wares. "Alte Zachen!" Old clothes! An old man pushing a cart sings up towards the windows in which he hopes prospective buyers and sellers wait. And down the street I hear the clip clopping of hooves announcing the vegetable cart's arrival. Housewives with market bags on their arms hurry down to finger purple eggplants, fresh cucumbers, sun red tomatoes, while I am more interested in the patient old horse, shifting its weight from foot to foot, swatting at flies with an uncombed tail, while its owner haggles with customers. In the summer, an Arab boy with a wagon full of fat watermelons rides down our street announcing his wares. "Watermelon on the knife!" His guttural cries an invitation to a royal treat. His knife glistens as he cleaves the sweet fruit, still warm from the fields, a wet sucking noise like a deep sigh coming from ruby bellies as he pulls out perfect red triangles on the tip of his blade.

Down the street iron cages are lifted from store-fronts, the butcher shop already surrounded by the meowing of hungry cats, their bodies too thin for their own fur which hangs from them like hand-me-down pelts. Over head, helicopters like fat metallic beetles churn across the sky, and from my room I know they are carrying wounded soldiers if their sound disappears towards Haifa, where the hospital will be waiting to put them back together. By afternoon our street has earned its nap, siesta time when everything shuts down, and children are told to be quiet in loudly whispered warnings. Now nothing is heard save the rustling of Eucalyptus trees in the breeze, muted conversations behind closed doors; a fretful child refusing sleep. When our neighborhood has had its rest teapots whistle and dishes clatter, welcoming friends for afternoon sweets. Children chase and shriek in the gardens, car engines tick their cooling down song, housewives bang pots and set tables, their heads craning out windows to call children in for supper. Shutters are lowered against the gathering dusk as crickets croon their lullabies. This is the music I learn to love, the music of my heart.

Hands

On an Israeli Bus

I can't take my eyes off the hands gripping the bus strap above me. They belong to a woman who is swaying with the dips and bumps of the road, as she hangs on and waits for her bus stop. They are sculpted, her hands, dark clay and ropy veins, their grip vise-like, determined. My grandmother's hands are also strong, a surgeon's hands, but they are elegant, ringed, as they hover with a cigarette neatly clasped between two fingers, or even when they're stained purple from the mercurochrome she dabs on patients' wounds. Everyone else in the family, men included, has delicate hands, long tapered fingers built for making music, turning pages. I am always asked to show my hands to people, my mother's evidence that I too, come from good stock, aristocracy. And when I spend the night at a classmate's house, she holds my hand during a thunderstorm and won't let go because it is so soft, she says. I'm warned to play ball with care, so as not to break the hands that will astound the world one day. Keep out of the sun, the wind, the cold, and never garden without gloves, my mother instructs. When we visit my uncle, father's brother, I look for my hands in his three daughters. Instead I see large, thick fingers with blunt broad nails. Hands that bake sweet cakes in their narrow kitchen, hands that play silly songs on the old piano, pinch the number of years I've turned on any given birthday. "Peasant hands," my mother calls them, disdain in her voice, and I secretly wish to be that too. Tonight on the bus ride home, I gaze at this woman's hands and I know what I want mine to be like. They are strong, willful, and confident. They are beautiful.

In My Father's Garden

My father is teaching me how to pull weeds, frowning his disapproval if I leave the roots in the ground. "Make sure you get it all so they don't come back," he teaches, and I try harder, not wanting to disappoint. I grab hold of the green tufts and gently tug until I hear the earth give way and the stubborn roots release their hold with a reluctant tear. If I knew my father wouldn't check, I would leave them all to grow as they please, the inexplicable sadness I feel at their demise no longer bothering me. I love the wild vines that creep uninvited into trees, their leaves mingling with their host, their flowers dripping in unexpected places. I silently root for the struggling seedling, pushing its way out of a crack in the sidewalk, demanding its own place in the world. These unwanted plants come equipped, as if they knew they would be doing battle. They fight with an impressive stubbornness, their thorns and tendrils meant to exhaust all but the most persistent of gardeners. I am always happy to let them win. When the loofah gourds we grow on the back fence hang dry from the vines, their missile-like bodies are oddly light as I gather them in the folds of my shirt. My job is to sort the seeds from the chaff, rubbing the papery skins between my fingers and watching them dance away with the breeze. They may be outcasts, but they swirl away on filmy wings, the whole world beneath them as they disappear.

Eman

Israel, 1977

My mother has brought home a little girl from *Tamra*, the Arab village where she works as a nurse. I've seen Eman before, running errands through unpaved streets, her bare feet coated with a fine layer of dust. I've sat with her on the cement floor in her mother's house, where we were invited to eat warm disks of Pita bread just baked. Her mother cleans around the nurses' station, offering steaming sweet tea she pours into thick glasses for the busy staff. Now her daughter sits at our table, her dinner plate perched on her small lap until my mother explains that it belongs on the table where she returns it with a sidelong glance for reassurance from me. That evening my mother draws Eman a bath, fills it with shiny bubbles that make her shriek with delight, quickly erasing the look of suspicion that had been in her eyes. Come nightfall she sleeps in my room, wearing a pair of my pajamas and hugging a doll I tell her she may keep. And the next day we take her to the beach, where she stands facing the Mediterranean she has never seen. I watch as she sinks her toes into the warm sand before she runs to the water's edge, retreating in fear as the waves roll in and lick her feet. That night, we giggle in our beds, our sun-warmed skin cool against crisp sheets. Her limited Hebrew and my complete lack of Arabic do not stop us from behaving like typical little girls. The next day when my mother returns her to her village, Eman yells at her mother, fury in her voice. She wants a bath like ours, a big bed with feathery pillows; the sea to play in. I wonder how her mother reacts, whether she stares helpless, or if she is angered at what my mother has caused. This piece of the story is not part of my mother's narrative.

Months later, the nurses' station is burned to the ground on a day my mother happens to be away. Angry villagers demonstrating their frustration over that which they cannot have, something even a child can understand. This time, despite my mother's absence from the scene, her description includes the group of Arab women standing on a rooftop across from the burning station, yelling "Death to Jews!" Among them is Eman's mother.

Year of Absence

The household is turned upside down, rooms emptied and prepared for the family of strangers who will be renting our home for a year. Only five days left until our trip to America, where father has been invited to teach once again. I've packed my Barbie dolls, bathing suit and books. Mother will see to the rest. All our friends and relatives are calling and visiting before we leave, inviting us to eat with them since our dishes are in boxes, and our furniture stored away in father's study which will remain locked until we return. The house feels strange, familiar but not, like the first night we ever spent in it, when the walls still smelled of fresh paint and the air was misty from *Fleet*, the bug spray my mother generously applied against the outlandishly large winged roaches dive-bombing through the open screens. We all slept in the living room on folding cots. Butterflies had fluttered in my stomach then as well, morning arriving too quickly, bringing my first day at a new school along with it.

But now the emptiness is filled with friendships made over the past three years, connections that will be put on hold, stretched thin but never torn over the distance we will travel. Sara is given a key to our house, and with it permission to watch another family whose movements will become part of her daily routine. And what amazes me most is just that, the fact that daily routines will continue, even when we are gone; Sara watching and reporting to the other gossips at the local kiosk. Ronit walking to school with Iris down the street instead of with me.

Field trips to the catacombs where bats fly so close you can feel the air moving against your face from their leathery wings. Sara's husband, Miron, will go fishing one afternoon only to return with the greatest fishing story he's ever told, the scar on his leg the only proof of the shark he fought off while we were gone. And while I am in California being introduced to a show called *Happy Days*, my immediate life goal a need for a black leather jacket, Egyptian president, Anwar Sadat will land at the airport from which I leave, and meet Israel's prime minister with whom he discusses peace.

Mother says it's only for a year, but she doesn't understand what can happen in that span of time. She says I'll make friends in America, and she's right, I do. A very blonde and pale skinned girl named Karen becomes my confidante; teaches me all about the game of jacks and introduces me to trolls which fascinate me with their colorful hair, even more unruly than my own. We will save our allowances until we have enough to buy these impish toys, both of us at the door of the shop the very morning they are delivered. Her mother will welcome me into their home, a lemon colored house with perfectly trimmed hedges and a parlor in which I am not invited to sit. And in the year her daughter and I spend in each other's company, I never learn Mrs. Adams' first name, unlike Ronit's mother who will always be Esti to me. When it is time for me to fly back home, Karen promises to write but stops after three letters and I never see her again when I return. This is the same year my mother discovers garage sales, an American pastime that sends her out of our rented house on Mulberry lane, and all around town for hours each Saturday morning, in search of bargains with which she furnishes our rooms.

This place in which I am a temporary resident will leave its imprint upon me in many ways. The television I watch voraciously fills my head with ideas of what being beautiful means on the American side of the world. I will insist that my hair needs to be as straight as the hair of the models I see parading across the screen during every commercial break.

My mother who knows nothing about hair products buys a box of Clairol at the local grocery store, and while I'm seated on top of the wooden table in our back yard, my curls will be transformed into sheets of flattened hair, my scalp hot and burning as my mother rereads the instructions she must have surely misunderstood. She buys this product at the same store where later she returns a bottle of root beer, believing that the strange drink must certainly be spoiled to taste like that.

This is also the year for learning kickball during P.E., and my English will improve enough to allow me to stand on a stage in front of all the sixth grade classes, and give a report on Israel. I am the only Israeli in the entire school when the United Nations day takes place and we all have to represent a country. A classmate chooses Israel as her country, too. But having a Jewish stepfather married to her Italian mother isn't nearly good enough as being born in the Holy land like me. Another student makes fun of a shirt I choose to wear to school one day, even though back home it seemed to be the fashion, and during lunch I'll have to explain that those large crackers I'm eating are called *matza* bread and that I have them because I'm Jewish and it's Passover.

But because we never stay long enough, my character plays a minor role in the drama of the American lives I briefly share. Not like here, in this room filled with friends and family that I am about to leave, where I am part of the colorful quilt draped over our neighborhood. My name will be called on the first day of school, and other students will *know* that I am coming back, that I am part of the forty heads that make up the family that is our class, all of us moving together from one grade to the next like some great beast the teachers dread. And even though I am forever remembered as that well-mannered girl whose family travels back and forth like migrating birds, those I leave behind on this side of the world will be watching the skies for my return.

* * *

Tucson, Arizona, 1978

We don't always end up in California when we leave the Middle East behind. In the summer of my twelfth year we spend one unforgettable month in Arizona, driving through a very different desert landscape than the one I had grown accustomed to. Unlike the predictability of the stark Judean desert, the scenery speeding past contains unusual surprises. On the other side of the car windows appear strange looking plants my father says are Saguaros, their fat arms and thick trunks covered in needle sharp spikes as they point toward cloudless blue skies. My father pulls the station wagon over to the side of the road, where I open the car door to be greeted by a wave of dry heat that rolls over me as if an oven door has swung wide and pushed me in; Nothing like the wet warmth back home, drenching laundry forgotten on the line overnight. While my mother remains in the car, prone to migraines in such heat, my brother and I walk through sand to meet one of these impressive sentinels up close, my father explaining how they store water in their fleshy limbs before reaching out and gently placing his palm on the majestic plant, bringing it away without a scratch. "Nice fella," he croons to the impassive giant as I watch in admiration.

We will be spending the next few weeks in a house tucked into the desert's flank, unseen until we turn the bend and there it is, camouflaged so as not to disturb the natural surroundings.

My father has been hired to teach one summer session at the University of Tucson and we will be staying in the house of his colleague, a tall Lebanese man who happens to be married to a Jewish woman whose five foot frame is topped by a halo of peroxide blond hair that looks like spun sugar. They greet us at the entrance to their hacienda style home, inviting us to come in from the furnace heat of the afternoon and into the frosty chill of air conditioning, goose bumps dotting my arms from the sudden change in climate. In our house in Israel air conditioning will not be introduced for another few years and then it will be piped through my brother's room and into my parents' bedroom, where we will all pile into their bed to cool off on especially unbearable days.

Before the colleague and his family take off to cooler regions, a move we only later understand, their very American looking children show us their rooms, my brother welcomed by the boy into a football fantasy he fails to appreciate, while the daughter invites me into a pink and white fairy tale which makes me think of frosted cupcakes and thrills me to no end. The house stretches almost imperceptibly over three levels, cool Mexican tiles leading at a gradual slope from the bedroom I will be occupying at the furthest end, to the arched entryway which opens to an exotic wonderland. Cacti of all shapes and sizes flower in brilliant colors, hot pink and fiery orange blossoms adorning their tops like gaudy crowns, while minute quails skitter behind their mother, feathered heads bobbing in their frenzied hurry. Small fuzzy rabbits hop past, completing the wonderland feeling I have had since our arrival. The occupants inside the house seem equally magical to me, relaxed in their banter with their parents, at ease in their wholesome good looks and the plenty of their surroundings which do not seem to impress them as they do me. Their mother suggests we shower after our long and

dusty drive, and offers an armful of thick, fluffy towels, refer-
ring to them as thirsty towels, such an unusual description that
I immediately store it to be used at a later date. Alongside this
mental note I must also make room for my mother's most recent
reprimand, since in reply to our hostess' calling of my name I
dared to answer with a "What!" from down the hall, instead of
the more proper "Yes", a mistake my mother does not hesitate to
point out in front of our new acquaintances. Spun sugar gives
an approving nod at my mother's child rearing skills while her
children roll their eyes and I wish I could too.

After leaving us with a list of instructions regarding the
house and two dogs we will be minding, the family heads out
the door that very night so much luggage going with them that if
I didn't know any better, I'd think they were never coming back.
We sit at their round kitchen table to read the list, pausing briefly at the entry warning to keep the dog food container sealed
tightly against Kangaroo rats, visions of monstrous rodents immediately filling my imagination. (Within days my father purchases humane traps then drives out into the desert with the
one he finds tripped one morning to release the creature, only to
discover the trap empty.) The handful of cups scattered around
the rim of the round fireplace in the middle of the living room
turn out to be strategically placed to catch rain water from the
leaks they have yet to fix, and not proof of slovenly housekeeping
as we first believed. The list also warns against rattle snakes in
the garden, and suggests we check our shoes and our beds before
occupying either, since scorpions have been known to crawl into
both. By the time we reach the end of the list I am not so certain
that this is where I want to stay.

The next day's visit to the Tucson Desert museum only
reinforces my fears. There in the manufactured dimness of a
cave-like room I see Vampire bats for the first time, perched on

branches behind thick glass, small bowls of what appears to be blood beneath them. I learn about the poisonous spiders that are common to the region and add them to the list of creatures to look out for during my evening preparations for bed. My nights are now filled with anxiety, sending me out of the fairy tale room and into the shadowy hallway which stretches menacingly into the furry dark where anything could be lying in wait. It does not help that in a room close to the entrance is a collection of Kachina dolls our hostess proudly showed us when we arrived, explaining that they were masked spirits of the Hopi tribe. I found their ominous carvings and odd faces disturbing, their presence down the hall causing shivers down my spine. I end my nightly excursions in the master bedroom where my parents sleep; a room I must reach by climbing a set of wrought iron spiral stairs and crossing a balcony suspended over the sunken living room. My walk comes to a stop at the side of their bed where I hover above their sleeping forms, until my mother jolts into wakefulness with a sharp intake of breath at finding me silently standing there. She does not get angry but she sends me back to my room, voicing an almost awed surprise that despite my fears I choose to wander alone in the darkness of the slumbering house rather than stay in the safety of my bed.

It is on one of these nights that I find my parents' bed empty, my mother making strange suffering sounds from the bathroom while my father is in the process of lacing his shoes. A migraine she had been battling all day had finally gotten the best of her and as a last resort my father was going to take her to a hospital he noticed on his early drives to the university campus, sending him out of the house at dawn each morning.

"Go wake your brother and get dressed," my father instructs.

I hurry back down the staircase, sliding across the tiled floor until I reach my brother's room and shake him into wakefulness.

Within minutes we are back in the hallway, watching as my father escorts my mother towards the door, her face pale as she attempts a smile in our direction. Even in this obviously weakened condition she refuses to admit what she considers defeat, smiling her embarrassment at having caused this disruption in our ordered lives. We head out the door, the night air surprisingly cool after the day's impossible heat which kept us reluctantly indoors, the dark desert sky scattered with sparkling stars, jewels on black velvet. We climb into the station wagon, my mother's head reclined, eyes closed, missing this spectacular night show I almost feel guilty for enjoying at her expense. I feel somehow responsible for her misery, blaming myself for her disrupted sleep as a result of my nightly fears. But the beauty of the night is too overwhelming and I revel in the sense of adventure with which I am filled as my father speeds down the empty desert road.

After an interminable wait in a small florescent lit room, my eight year old brother curled on the wooden bench at my side, my mother is released, diagnosed with Valley Fever, something I could not possibly have had a hand in. She has been injected with a substance that renders her sleepy and calm, my father leading her back to the car, my brother and I in tow, too tired to ask questions.

Before our stay in this desert wonderland comes to an end, we are still in for more surprises. Since my mother's diagnosis we have been captives inside this desert abode, only allowed out into the enclosed garden where my curiosity causes me to reach for a harmless looking plant covered in what looks like fine hair. Within seconds my palm and fingers are coated in thousands of tiny needles, rendering my hand numb and keeping my mother occupied while she attempts to extract the miniscule needles with a pair of tweezers. While doing so she tells a story of the time when, new to Israel at the age of thirteen, she had peeled her first prickly pear then licked the knife with which she did so ("Never lick knives," she warns as an aside), unaware of the fruit's protective covering.

Later that evening, my hand still throbbing from the prickly encounter, we listen to the news as the weather man announces that a monsoon is on its way, declaring the exact time we should expect its arrival and the duration of its stay. We all wait in anticipation, dubious at the confidence of his prediction until we hear a clap of thunder, followed by a display of lightning, the likes of which none of us had or ever would be witness to again. Bolts of electricity mythological in proportion rip through the night skies, followed by torrential rains which start impressively at the exact time the weatherman had predicted. Every thunderous explosion sends the two dogs scurrying under the kitchen table, howling their distress while we watch, glued to the windows, astonished at this spectacular display which ends precisely at its scheduled time. And as our hosts' list promised, the cups around the fireplace begin to fill as thin rivulets of rain make their way down the chimney pipe's sides. This storm seems fitting as our stay comes to an end, my father's teaching assignment concluded and our departure from the United States impending. Despite its magical qualities I am relieved at our approaching departure from this strange terrain, eager to return to deserts in which I anticipate nothing more than tan colored camels dotting the sandy landscape and swarthy Bedouin offering my mother riches in return for her daughter's hand in marriage. There is nothing to fear in the familiar Judean desert, while the Sonoran landscape has overwhelmed us foreigners with its deadly beauty.

*   *   *

Israel, 1979

This time around Israel gets to hold on to us for two years before my mother hears America calling again. Once more I am reintroduced to my neighborhood and friends, to being an Israeli. I nearly pull it off, my classmates used to my frequent disappearing act, until I use a word that is no longer considered cool and watch their faces break into wide grins at my outdated vocabulary. This is seventh grade and I cannot show that they have upset me by reminding me that I do not completely belong. Yet I make a mental note to remove the archaic word and replace it with the newer version once I figure it out.

Back in my room on the third floor of our *Villa*, surrounded by the trappings of our American possessions, I look out the window onto familiar Israeli landscapes. Solar water heaters still dot the rooftops of neighboring apartment buildings. Laundry lines sag under the weight of drying clothes. Comforting sounds of neighbors float through my open window, pots banging, a kettle shrilly whistling its steamy cry. A radio announcer's excited voice gains momentum as he gives a play-by-play of a soccer game, the roar of victorious fans in the background. I have missed these sounds during the year we have been away in a country where the silence of an afternoon is rarely broken by Americans who value their peace and privacy. I take comfort in discovering that nothing much has changed in my absence other than the Eucalyptus trees we planted against the fence before we left. Like me, they have gained some height over the past year, their long slender leaves rustling in the breeze, branches reaching for the skies.

The Stain

Israel, 1978

My mother is in her element. I have turned twelve, and my *bat mitzvah* party is just a few hours away, caterers like frenzied ants carrying trays of food, crisp linen tablecloths, sparkling wine glasses, steaming pots. Small round tables have appeared under the trees in our garden, like mushrooms after a rain, while from branch to branch hang wires bearing colorful lanterns which will soon bathe the greenery in magical light.

My father has disappeared altogether, his distaste for elaborate celebrations ignored by my mother's need for the dramatic. He suffers quietly through every birthday, his own included, while my mother begins the festivities at the first light of dawn. I still recall waking up to the shadowy outlines of gifts in my room, and my mother's eager face bent over mine, bursting into the birthday song, her eyes reprimanding anyone who wasn't showing enough enthusiasm. It never stopped there. Birthday breakfast was followed by cake; Birthday lunch, and cake. Birthday dinner, more cake. And a constant need to ensure that we were enjoying ourselves, that the gifts were appreciated, that the day was special enough, not just another ordinary day.

Today she has outdone herself and soon will come her confirmation in the shape of dozens of guests who will attest to her entertaining prowess. All I need to do is put on the dress purchased for the occasion, thank one and all for my gifts, and keep my hands out of her sight until the stains are successfully removed. The now fading purple splotches that covered my hands like a pair of berry colored gloves were the result of a science experiment gone wrong the day before. The biology teacher had most likely explained the effects of *Kali Permanganate* on skin, but her warnings had faded into the distance as I dropped the dark crystals in the liquid before me, watching the slow curl of violet tails swirl towards the bottom of the glass container. I wanted to feel those smoky ribbons, their regal color, my hands dipping into the water and fishing out the nearly dissolved crystals so I could drop them in again, make them repeat their watery dance before their magic wore off. By the time the teacher caught me in her sights the damage had been done. My hands were slowly darkening, my classmates awed into unusual silence.

My mother had not been pleased. "Why now? Why today?" She questioned when I arrived from school, shaking her head in disbelief at my bad timing, her lips a thin disapproving line. I didn't know how to explain how my heart had leapt at the unexpected secret contained in those deceivingly mediocre specks on my desk. How they flowered before my eyes and asked to be touched. I had spent the rest of the afternoon scrubbing until my hands felt raw, the stubborn dye slowly fading under the persistence of water, soap and my mother's determination. There was a moment when she suggested I wear gloves to the party, to hide the embarrassment of such hands. But the royal smudges gave way, and now the only reminder was their dark outline soaked in around each of my nails, and a strange sadness I felt at the return of my skin to its regular unimpressive color.

Dusk is settling between the apartment buildings surrounding our garden, softening their gray cinder walls until they disappear into the background. Classical music is spilling from the balcony above, and our first guests are arriving. Festivities rarely begin early on this side of the world, partygoers waiting for the heat of the day to dissolve before venturing out. Among the invited is family having traveled from Tel Aviv, a negligible distance in American terms, while an entire day's outing for the aunts, uncles and cousins now unfolding out of their cars, stretching and rubbing their muscles. My mother greets one and all, excusing herself to answer the jangling of our telephone, demanding to be answered despite the stream of people making their way into our courtyard. I am left with my father's colleague, a short round-faced man everyone refers to as Perlberg, who offers me a small gift-wrapped box and waits expectantly for me to open it before him. Unlike the growing pile of books and sheet music I have already graciously accepted from guests clearly concerned with my educational wellbeing, this present promises something different and I am eager to learn its contents. So is its presenter, who helps me with the wrapping I am trying not to tear, then steps back to take in my reaction. The simple white box contains soft cotton in which is nestled the most beautiful necklace I had ever received. At the end of a delicate silver chain hangs a cylindrical piece of polished sea glass, its pale green blue shades trapping waves and drawing my finger to feel its smooth flanks. I look up to thank Perlberg, the delight in his eyes at the offering's effect matching my own at receiving it.

"It's thousands of years old," he tells me as he offers to clasp it around my neck. "It was found at an archeological dig," he continues, as I turn back to face him now wearing this piece of history. "Thank you" I whisper, my shyness taking over as I leave his side and run into the house to show my mother who has not returned since going in to answer the call.

The phone is missing from its stand on the second floor landing, and my eyes follow its curly cord as it wraps around the wall and into the narrow guest bathroom where it disappears behind the door left slightly ajar. I can hear my mother's muffled voice from within, the few words of Polish I have picked up from years of listening to my mother and grandmother not enough to let me understand. I stand rooted to the floor, trying to figure out who could be on the other side of the line, since everyone we know has been invited and is now seated in the garden below. While I am still lost in thought my mother emerges, the phone clasped to her chest, a strained look which she quickly attempts to erase from her face when she finds me standing there. "Who called?" I ask, as I watch her features intently, the hint of tears in her eyes making me suspicious. I had seen this look before, a rapid adjustment to protect me from a frightening truth. Last time she had used it at the beach, when she decided I was old enough to swim with her out to the wooden raft, a popular destination for strong swimmers and teenagers trying to impress their dates. A jellyfish had stung her as we made our way. They floated all around us, their pale lavender domes gently bumping into our sides, misleading with their soothing color. I ignored their tentacles, just as I had pushed out of my mind all thoughts of what may be contained in the depths yawning darkly below me. I was determined to reach that raft, my mother's tight smile and everything I didn't know protecting me from panic.

Now once again she pretended all was well. "It was just your aunt Ula from Berlin calling to wish you a happy birthday." I knew she was lying, recognizing the unnatural tightness of that smile, but I was still too young to question my mother's version of the truth. She promised to rejoin the party and sent me back down stairs, my new necklace forgotten as the sound of guests welcomed me back to their happy midst.

It isn't until the next morning that I am finally told about the call. By then my mother has been long gone, the neighbor having driven her to the airport where she already boarded a plane to Austria where her father lay dying. I slept unknowingly through it all.

The house is strangely silent, most traces of yesterday's festivities cleaned away. The garden has returned to its disenchanted greenery, the grey apartments back in sharp relief against the blue sky. The carport that had served as last night's bar now holds nothing but the old blue Fiat and a handful of tiny, nearly translucent Geckos, watching me from their perch on the walls. How simple it was to turn the ordinary into remarkable; and how easily the deceptively tranquil held unexpected secrets. Like the happy Perlberg, who in just a few years will call a cab into which he will then load himself, a ladder and a rope and ask the driver to drop him off in the forests of the Carmel where he will later hang himself.

I make my way back into the house, up the stairs and to my room. All traces of the magic in which my hands had briefly dipped are gone.

While We Were Sleeping

Israel, April 1979

I am not taught to hate. Not when the Arab villagers burn down the nurses' station where my mother works, the women who had once held their newborn babies trapped under a table inside. Not when I am ten and barely understand where this place called Uganda is, and why all the adults around me are talking about the Entebbe rescue mission and some man called Idi Amin. My parents will later take me to the film someone made about the hijacking of the Air France Airbus, and for nights I will replay the scene in which the terrorists free the French crew and passengers who are not Jewish, and make all the people with Israeli names move to the other side of the room. I can picture our family among them, the hijackers trying to pronounce my name, my mother angered at the injustice of it all. I suddenly understand why she always makes me tuck the gold chain with the Star of David medallion into my shirt when we fly across the world. I also cannot seem to erase the image of the young Lt. Col. Yonatan Netanyahu, who led the rescue mission. He was leading rescued hostages out of the airport when the bullet found him and he fell to the ground, just like the flowers his father dropped on the Israeli tarmac when he came to welcome his son home and was told he was dead.

Three years later I see the horror on adults' faces when they discover what took place not far from us while we slept. It was a regular Sunday morning, the first day of the work and school week, when four men snuck into Israel in a rubber boat, making their way to an apartment building just like the ones that lined our street. They broke into the Haran family's apartment where they took a father and his four-year old girl hostage, while the mother hid in a crawl space with a two-year old daughter. She knew that they would be discovered if the child made a sound, so she kept her hand over her mouth to muffle the little girl's whimpering. And while her husband and older daughter were murdered on the beach, she accidentally smothered her baby, and in a matter of minutes lost her entire family while we slept.

All during the summer months that followed, father away teaching in America while mother lay awake listening for intruders and planning our escape route, my eyes searched the horizon every time we went to the beach. I used to wade in, turn my back to the waves, and wait for a large one to sweep me back to shore, my biggest fear the lavender jellyfish that floated around me on my salty ride. Now I kept my eyes trained on that distant horizon, half expecting to see a small rubber boat carrying men angry enough to kill, the threat of a salty sting forgotten in the face of a much greater danger. So when I turned eighteen and the army put an Uzi in my hands and trained me to use it, I was ready to do so. Not because I hated, but because I was being raised in a country where it was being made painfully clear that others hated us.

Mrs. Kaminsky

Israel, Summer 1979

I spend many summer mornings in my grandmother's company, in the passenger seat of her white Volkswagen bug
hanging on to dear life as she speeds through the narrow
Haifa streets, confident in her driving skills as she is in all other
aspects of her life. The white dividing line between lanes is often
ignored when she needs more space, and if parking is not available when she requires it, my grandmother parks on the sidewalk, her physician's permit dangling from the mirror, protecting her from police officers' wrath. When I was young enough
to barely see over the dashboard she would instruct me to hold
on to the handle jutting out from the glove compartment, and I
would pretend to drive the car along with her, the two of us an
unbeatable team racing to our various destinations. The glove
compartment itself held one of my favorite treats in a round silver tin filled with cellophane wrapped mints, each one a perfect
square of light blue candy that reminded me of ice cubes. When
I wasn't accompanying her to work in the small clinic in which
her name preceded her like an exaltation we ran errands and I
would be introduced to various trades people, all of them my
grandmother's former patients, all of them eternally grateful for
whatever procedure she had performed. There was the furrier, a
grizzled old man whose small shop was dark and smelled of animal pelts whose fur hung in various stages of completion, awaiting wealthy clients whose shoulders they would adorn at the
next opera or concert. My grandmother was having a coat made
for my mother's birthday (not a mink because, she explained,

my mother was too young), and was stopping in to check on its progress, the Russian shopkeeper retrieving the fur and allowing her to inspect his work before she swept back out into the summer light with me in tow, grateful to be out of a place that smelled like so much death.

Today though, our errand involves me directly since the purpose of our outing is to purchase a new bathing suit, and according to my grandmother there is only one place where this can be done. We head towards *Hadar*, Hebrew for splendor, the section of the mountain between the upper and lower city of Haifa, overlooking the port and bay. Small shops of various sorts line the busy streets as my grandmother maneuvers the car between two others, leaving it parked at a rakish tilt, its two left wheels on the sidewalk. We make our way past a shoe store and a bakery, the smell of leather and pastries wafting out and mingling as we hurry past to the shop where my new bathing suit awaits. Barely in the door of the establishment and we are greeted by a small, rotund woman who hurries towards us with quick mincing steps, her hands clasped in delight at the sight of my grandmother gracing her shop.

"Dr. Henner! Such an honor! How may I be of assistance?"

"Good morning Mrs. Kaminsky. We are here for a suit for my granddaughter, something very nice please." My grandmother's voice is kind if commanding; accustomed to giving orders and expecting they be fulfilled. She has worked hard all her life and expects no less from anyone else.

"Of course Dr. Henner, only the best for you and your granddaughter." Mrs. Kaminsky shifts her attention to me for the first time since we walked in, measuring with narrowed eyes that make me immediately self-conscious.

"Please follow me, I have beautiful new suits upstairs, we try." And she turns on her heel, surprisingly agile as she takes the narrow stairs, my grandmother and I following.

The summer heat has found its way to the second floor where the shop owner shows my grandmother to a chair, waving me into one of two curtained dressing rooms while she brings an assortment of bathing suits for me to try. I glance back at my grandmother, her thin legs crossed, her right hand clasping a cigarette, its smoke curling up towards her narrow face, the aquiline nose lending elegance to her already dignified features. I feel clumsy in comparison, my thirteen year old body painfully childlike as I undress and wriggle into the first tight fitting suit, wishing I could be as beautiful as the models in the photos adorning the walls of the shop, as sure of myself as my grandmother, waiting to see the results. But before I have had the chance to assess myself in the narrow dressing room mirror, the curtain is brushed aside and Mrs. Kaminsky is grasping one of my shoulders, tugging and adjusting straps as I stand horrified at this blatant invasion of my privacy.

"Good, good, you like? All made in Israel, best quality. I show others." Her small form presses against me as she prods and squeezes, clucking and commenting about breasts that are yet to arrive, hips that are still slim as a boy's, a faint odor of sweat and an overly sweet perfume making me slightly nauseous as she pushes me towards my grandmother for inspection. Yet my grandmother shakes her head in disapproval, and I am almost relieved, hoping that this means that my humiliation has ended. No such luck.

"No black bathing suits. She is too young to wear black." And with that I am shooed back in to try three more suits, all of which are closely examined by Mrs. Kaminsky and then my grandmother, before a red one is decided upon. By this point I am so eager to leave that I would have said yes to anything they selected.

Once downstairs, my grandmother pays for the new bathing suit, promising to return for future purchases and to bring me along as well. Yet by next summer I will be away from her in America, where we will soon learn that bathing suits must be bought while winter is still in the air, in large impersonal department stores in which dressing rooms have sturdy doors that lock from the inside, and generous mirrors that make everyone look good in the altered light. For years to come, Mrs. Kaminsky's ghost follows me into American dressing rooms, where I half expect the door to swing open and the commentary to begin. Of course nothing of the sort happens, and certainly no grandmother is sitting and smoking, waiting for me, and I leave with barely a glance from the dressing room attendant who has nothing to say about the choices I have made and the appropriateness of the black bathing suit I insist on buying.

Experiments

Israel, 8th Grade

My happiness at being returned to the familiar Israeli landscape and beginning a second uninterrupted year among friends is short lived, when another decision is made for me. Unimpressed with the Israeli school system, my parents decide to send me to another school, an experimental one where classes are conducted in the American style of teaching. This is a surprising move considering my mother's overprotective nature, since getting to the University of Haifa where this school is located involves two buses I will have to catch on my own, my younger brother in tow. I still have time to socialize with old classmates, but once again I stand out, and as I do when traveling between my two countries, I must split myself between two groups of friends, divide my loyalties and learn different ways.

This new group of eighth graders includes a handful of Americans whose parents have relocated to Israel, and a few students whose wildness amazes me as I sit politely observing their behavior. My parents were right about one thing; this school is certainly less traditional and regimented. In fact, no regiment seems to exist at all, and with the exception of the creative writing teacher who manages to briefly hold our attention, other instructors don't last the hour, and few bother to return. One teacher even shrieks her disapproval when a dark haired boy named Ronny climbs to the top of the door and swings, howling like a monkey. I spend the year socializing, our small group of about a dozen students offering an interesting mix of backgrounds and temperaments. From gossipy Eti, who rumor has it is the daughter of the school janitor and lives right under the classrooms in a tiny apartment, to Gilia who frowns her disgust at our juvenile behavior, her pale skin turning an angry red when she can't talk us out of our newest prank. We spend most of our time in the forest surrounding the university throwing tires we find off the mountain, catching small scorpions in glass jars, gossiping about the latest targets of our thirteen-year old crushes, and learning how to spit. At some point I make the mistake of revealing my infatuation for Tomer, a broad shouldered boy with hulking good looks. When I arrive at school the next morning, two girls drag me to the empty nurse's office, shoving me inside where I find Tomer already waiting; a bewildered look on his face.

"You're not coming out till you kiss!" The girls shriek and lock the door, leaving us to stare at each other across the narrow room. My stomach is churning and I seem to have forgotten how to breathe. From the look on Tomer's face his body isn't turning against him as is mine, a shy smile playing on his lips as he takes a careful step toward me. My brain adds itself to the list of malfunctioning body parts; all thought suspended as his face hovers inches from mine. He is close enough for me to notice the fine layer of dark fuzz that has recently appeared above his top lip.

"Do you want to? They told me that you said you like me, but you don't have to." His eyes are hopeful and one of his hands has found its way around my own. I don't know where to put the other one, backing into the nurse's examination table, making the paper stretched across its top like a thin skin crinkle against my shirt.

"Okay." My voice all but fails me as I whisper agreement, and Tomer must have heard because his lips are on mine, and this they seem to know how to do. Warmth floods my face and I am amazed at the softness of his lips. I feel myself smiling, deciding right then and there that kissing must be one of the best things I have ever done. I can't wait to get home and tell Ronit, and for the next few weeks I fill my diary with hearts, arrows carrying our initials plunged through their crimson centers. I forgive Eti and the other girls for watching us from the other side of the window to make sure we didn't cheat. I even forgive my parents for their decision to send me away from my old classmates, suddenly all for experimentation and lack of traditional schooling. After all, there is nothing like a first kiss.

Under Cover of Night

Israel, Summer 1980

We're headed for the airport, stretches of dark road swallowed in large gulps under the car's wheels as we speed through the night on our way out again. A loyal friend is at the wheel, giving up sleep to see us off on our ritual departure from this land that cannot seem to keep us. My face is glued to the window's glass, a last attempt to memorize a friend's familiar face; Mediterranean to my right, still shrouded in its misty quilt, banana groves on my left. Distant minarets dot the hills of Arab villages slumbering until a muezzin will call them to prayer, demanding that they sacrifice sleep for faith. "Allah U Akbar!" His night-veiled voice breaks into all of our dreams. Our leave-taking always happens at night, as if we are stealing away, afraid of being asked why we cannot stay. The routine is well-practiced by the time I have lost the sense of excitement for these nightly departures. The sight of our suitcases lined up by the front door where my father had dragged them the evening before, used to cause my breath to catch in my throat, the thought of America gleaming in the distance. Now all I want is to run out that door, turn left at the edge of the sidewalk, and sprint the short distance remaining between me and the parking lot under Ronit's bedroom window. I'll stand there and call up her name, the vulgar Israeli way mother's good breeding forbids. I'll send up her name like the incense smoke of offerings supplicants leave on temple altars. Neighbors will complain at the disturbance as Ronit's window shutters pull upwards, her head emerging as she wipes away sleep. Once she realizes it is me below, she waves me up the three flights of steps and I am allowed to stay, pick up where we left off, instead of heading towards a new house, new friends who will never know me like she does.

Instead, airport doors slide open as though expecting us, and we have left the darkness outside to be replaced by artificial lights in a world that never sleeps. People are hurrying past us, jockeying for position at terminal gates, lifting overstuffed luggage onto conveyor belts that slither away and swallow their holy land souvenirs. The routine is familiar, passports, tickets; the usual questions about our stay, our destination.

"Who packed your bags?"

"We did."

"Did you leave them unattended?"

"Of course not."

"Have you accepted any packages from strangers since your arrival in the terminal?"

"Certainly not," my mother answers a note of righteous indignation in her voice. I focus my attention on the crowds gathering behind us. An orthodox man in a long black coat, his wife and half dozen children in tow, off to be holy somewhere else. A young couple with love and excitement in their eyes, adventure in the tickets they clasp in their hands. A group of young men on the verge of military service, ink from their high school exams barely dry on their fingers, one last taste of freedom to enjoy before their country calls. And then there is us. Mother efficient and thin lipped as she handles officials, father tense; his dislike for this all too frequent exodus obvious in his pale face. My brother, too young to grieve for a land he does not feel deep down in his bones as I do; and me. Already wondering what is happening to all I left behind, hoping that the small envelope of passion flower seeds will go undetected through security, especially once we land in San Francisco where I know they have dogs that sniff people's luggage. These are not just any flower seeds, but ones right out of the purple globes hanging from the vines on Ronit's fence. We had watched them swell under the heat of the Mediterranean sun, waited for just the right moment to break them open and fish out the hard black seeds, drying them in time for this important move across the world. I check my pocket for the list of items friends and neighbors requested we bring back from America. *One jar, Tasters Choice coffee* for Sara, the neighbor across the courtyard. She comes for coffee every afternoon and swears it tastes better in our American cups. One pair Adidas size 13 for a cousin whose feet are outgrowing anything Israeli shoemakers seem to be able to create. *Sugarless gum for Ronit, any kind, doesn't matter.* Makeup – Maybelline for Tali who works miracles with a tiny brush and golden powder she sprinkles on her eyelids, glittering shutters coyly lowered when men are around. The list is long, but I tuck it back into my pocket since we are being ushered onto the plane, jostled and pushed by passengers more eager to leave than we must be. We are greeted by flight attendants in flawlessly tailored suits, their snowy white teeth smiling at us from beautiful faces in perfect makeup. Their hair looks as though they have just left the beauty parlor, blond waves encircling high cheekbones, silky curls falling where they are told. I become painfully aware of my own unruly hair, the absence of beauty products from my round Slavic face, and the sensible shoes and outfit mother set out for me the night before. "You need to be comfortable," she reasons when I complain, her own figure clad in a pant suit both confining and, I am certain of this, fire retardant from its stiff look. "You never know what could happen," visions of disaster in her green eyes, premonition of danger in her voice.

We settle back in our seats, morning slowly seeping into the plane's windows as I bend forward to catch a glimpse of my country waking up. That last glance always surprises me with its added luster, as if the land knows I am leaving and has draped itself in beauty I took for granted the day before. In my mind's eye I picture the glistening waves of the Mediterranean. Early morning joggers are crushing seashells under their feet as they run past scenery at which they no longer marvel. I can smell the warm sweet scent of bakeries, pastries displayed on trays like so many gleaming jewels. And in a few minutes, Jacob who owns the small grocery down the street will be rolling out the olive and pickle barrels, brine floating over their tops. I've seen him dip his arm and come up with the sour catch, weighing and wrapping the customer's request in smooth practiced moves.

But now the airplane's heavy door swings shut with hermetic finality, sealing out the sounds my country is made of. And once I lose sound, sight is quick to follow as the plane begins to roll away from the building where it was attached by a long umbilical corridor. *There's no reason to cry,* I try to convince myself, pressing the nails of my right hand into my palm to keep away the hot tears gathering behind my eyelids. Small half moons are left in my fisted hand as I turn my face to the window for a last glimpse of the building, silhouetted soldiers guarding from its rooftop. My father feigns sleep, my mother sits clutching the golden Madonna around her neck, and the plane gathers speed, swaying palms in the distance, waving goodbye. *Be back in a year,* I mouth into the oval pane, as we lose our connection with the ground and rise into the sky.

Toy Soldier

I am riding on the handlebars of Yanir's bicycle my eyes
squeezed shut so I won't see when we crash into parked cars
on the way to school. The wind is whipping my hair into
his face and he doesn't seem to mind, the drunken wobbling of
the bike demanding all his attention. I'm yelling for him to stop
because I don't like going so fast, but he ignores me because I'm
also laughing and he's a thirteen-year old boy with a girl on his
handlebars. When we were younger Yanir would come spend
time with me in the courtyard in front of my house. We played
in the old wooden shipping crate, the one my parents sent ahead
from America the last time we returned to Israel. We would play
with some of the plastic soldiers he brought, throwing them into
the dark cavern of the crate, daring each other to retrieve them.
He grabbed my wrist once, surprising me with his strength, and
with his small pointed face close to mine made me swear never
to tell *anyone* he played with a girl. "I'll kill you if you tell," he
said, and I believed him. He was small for his age, the other boys
in class always making fun. It didn't help when in fifth grade Yanir and I switched classes, he to sit in my chair learning to sew
and knit, while I took his place among the boys in carpentry.
An unprecedented move my mother initiated, appalled by the
Israeli school system's sexist practices. It also didn't help when he
panicked the morning the school nurse walked into our class, his
turn for shots arriving faster than he wanted. Before the nurse
finished calling out his name, Yanir took one step back and hit
his head on the cabinet behind him, knocking himself out cold

to the shrieks and jeers of classmates.

In boot camp years later as I am walking towards the dining hall, a large green truck carrying soldiers from the men's camp down the road comes rumbling by. And I'm willing to swear I see Yanir, there in the back of the truck, swaying with the movement of the vehicle, surrounded by tough looking soldiers. I call out and wave, but his eyes briefly meet mine, threatening once again not to give him away.

Ronit

Her hands are always clammy, and in a few years she'll be too heavy-chested and wide-hipped to become the dancer in her dreams. For now she walks in a permanent first position, and on the subway we take to the dance studio she reaches into her bag and pulls out her toe shoes, casually inspecting them while sending sidelong glances to see if any passengers are impressed. Unlike me, she's allowed to go out late and doesn't call home to say she got there. Perched on her bed, I watch her paint ink black mascara around almond shaped eyes. Her hennaed hair is wrapped in a bath towel, the mysterious *abuagella* hairstyle she does herself, tucked safely out of the way. It's nearing my curfew and by the time she's ready I'll have to go home. Sometimes after school, we climb up the three long flights to her apartment where I watch, awed, as she makes herself a hot meal. Steaming tea in glass mugs the color of dark honey, no house-keeper, nanny or mama to serve it. She can follow a recipe, throw salt over her left shoulder for luck, mop a floor, and put herself to bed. I can read *Quo Vadis* and make the piano sob Chopin, but I can't run downstairs with her when her boyfriend whistles from the parking lot under her bedroom window, and I won't be joining her at the local discotheque to dance away my shyness. Her family crowds in front of the television every Friday afternoon; hanging on each word of the Arab soap opera erupting in guttural bursts of tragedy. I don't speak Arabic, no matter how much the teacher yells at the class to pay attention. Ronit's father, whose dark skin and kind eyes make me feel like one of the family, tries to explain the swirling Arab letters to us at the tiny desk tucked into the corner of their kitchen. I smile, pretending to understand, not wanting to disappoint.

Years later after I abandon my friend, I will climb those three flights again and knock on that door, my heart beating wildly. Before I am allowed to see my past, I can already imagine the tiny apartment. Above the sofa hangs the ornate, gilded picture frame surrounding black velvet on which a gypsy woman swirls her red skirts. Across the room on the opposite wall is a shelf holding the large candle shaped like lovers, their eternal love captured in wax, the turtle shell, its empty hole a hungry mouth, and the miniature rocking chair Ronit's father made out of clothespins, the Barbie doll I brought her when we were nine sitting in it, wearing her perpetual grin. Ronit had waited an entire summer for the promised doll, gathering in the carport among a handful of other neighborhood friends on the very night of our return, suitcases unzipped right then and there in the car's trunk to dole out gifts from America. The echo of my knock still hanging in the stairwell, Ronit's mother will open the heavy armored door, shriek once, and squeeze me as if I were her own child, her slight frame uncannily strong for such a wisp of a woman. Her father, his shoulders slightly more stooped, will kiss me on both cheeks and I will be home.

For Ronit

You took my hand there in the schoolyard, and made me safe. Rode the train with me up the mountain to dance and dream; my dark sister. Worlds apart, thick as thieves, my tune Chopin waltzes, your television spilling Arab drama on Friday afternoons; You with the hips and the beat, me with the books and the left feet, together dancing to an invisible living room audience. You stayed behind while I flew away, leaving you with one husband, then another, tired from too many children and not enough dancing, still holding my hand.

*   *   *

Every Tuesday afternoon, Ronit and I set out for ballet. The dance studios are located in Haifa, in an old building called the Rothschild house that holds the city's largest theater. We have to start out early to catch a bus followed by a ride on the underground train that carries us to Mount Carmel, a different world from the suburbs where our families live. Once in awhile, if the weather is especially bad, Ronit's father will drive us in his covered truck, where we each stretch out on a narrow bench in the back, holding on for dear life. But the bouncing of the truck combined with the exhaust fumes that seep in make me sick and I prefer the excitement of a big city without an adult watching our every move. Sometimes I think the ride to ballet is more enjoyable than the classes themselves, but I keep this thought to myself so as not to sound ungrateful. I don't tell my mother that I feel ridiculous in tights and leotard that cling and scratch, my underwear showing no matter how far up I hike it. I don't tell her that I prefer dancing in our own living room on lazy Saturday afternoons, the Persian rug rolled to the side, the room washed in sunlight pouring through the wide open window, Ronit and I swirling around the floor to the sound of my record of *Swan Lake*. I don't tell her that I dread lining up in the corner of the dance studio, waiting my turn to pirouette across the room while everyone watches my awkward attempts to stay in a straight line. And when all the girls are fitted for toe shoes, I nod agreement when asked by the woman kneeling before me if mine seem like the right size, thinking that the pain I feel is how it is supposed to be from what I overheard the older girls saying in the dressing room, their toes blistered and bleeding. Ronit and I stay in the dressing room longer than necessary to change, just so we can hear the older dancers talking, hoping for a piece of information we can use. Like the day we discover that their underwear doesn't show like ours because they don't bother to wear any under their tights. We are shocked into respectful and awed silence.

And still, the sights and sounds I collect on our way to class stay with me far beyond the instructions of the old dance teacher, Ms. Schubert, her cane striking the floor to the beat of the piano an old accompanist plays in the corner of the cavernous room. Once our bus arrives in Haifa's downtown, Ronit and I hurry past shop fronts where mannequins show off the latest fashions, kiosks whose shelves are lined with colorful candy, awnings strung with porn magazines, attached by clothes pegs to covers on which women in startling positions leer at passersby. I wonder if they too had mothers who made them go to ballet classes. At the mouth of the underground our pace quickens as we strain to hear whether the train has arrived, a rush of warm air greeting us as we race down the steps into the musty smell of the tunnel, past whichever musician has lain claim to the busiest corner. The deafening roar of the train excites me, its bright light growing larger as it sweeps past us, a metallic snake cutting through the mountain and carrying us to the more civilized regions above.

The last stretch of freedom before entering the dance studios takes us past the zoo, alongside sidewalk cafes where older couples are enjoying coffee and cakes, and near a kiosk where ice cream bars are sold, neither Ronit nor I able to resist. We have no more than a five-minute walk to the studio, and I make short shrift of the lemony ice I choose, unlike Ronit who still has half a pineapple flavored popsicle left when we arrive at the door, risking the dance teacher's anger at seeing her students indulging in sweets. Rumor has it that Ms. Schubert used to weigh the girls before each practice, and I wonder if this was done in front of the whole class, like the nurse who comes in at school to check for lice and give shots while everyone watches. Ronit does not make it past the first door, the hand she tries to hide behind her back and the guilty look on her face summoning the dance mistress into the hall.

"What are you holding behind your back?" Ms. Schubert's thin frame is wrapped in a black leotard, its long skirt flowing and falling freely, unimpeded by any extra folds or layers that the rest of us are taught to suck in. Ronit's mouth attempts an answer but none follows as she brings her hand forward, pineapple rivulets making their sticky way down her arm.

"You should know better than to add to the fat you already have," and she gestures with her cane towards Ronit's hips, the kind I wish I had along with my nonexistent breasts.

"I will have to speak with your mother. Now wash up and get ready for class." And with that she glides back down the hallway, her cane emphasizing each step on the cement floor as she leaves us staring after her, Ronit with a stricken look on her face, while I do my best to glare at her receding back. Ronit's dream is to become a dancer, to travel to America with me and be discovered. It was my mother who suggested she should take up dancing, Ronit's head filled with nothing else ever since. Unlike my friend, I see no purpose in hours of bending and stretching at the bar, putting up with eccentric teachers, one stranger than the next. My muse is not to be found in dancing. Instead I turn to the books that line my shelves, words that fill me with ideas of who to be and how to sound. I fall in love with movies as well; sitting mesmerized, tears welling, throat constricting at the wonders flashing on the screen before me. I watch as Charlie Bucket soars unharmed through a ceiling in a glass elevator, the world at his feet. I hold my breath as Jane and Michael jump into a chalk drawing, emerging in their finery in a world of wonder and imagination. I envy Maria as she races up an Austrian mountain, her arms flung out to embrace the day. If only I could feel that free, that far from my mother's rules, from dance teachers who insist I focus on a spot I cannot see on a wall that pens me in.

I dance in America as well, where polite, pretty dance instructors hardly leave an impression, smiling their approval no matter how awkwardly I tap my way across the stage. Although there is one diminutive woman who believes I have "lots of stamina and an artistic nature" while convinced that close friendships with the other girls have little chance to flourish since they have worked together for years and my time with them has been brief. She also adds that I need to lift my eyelashes and sparkle, information she conveys to my mother in handwritten notes on thin paper she refers to as progress reports. Back in Israel again, where they don't teach how to sparkle, the final straw is the small muscular chain smoker from whom I take lessons with a group of girls in the living room of his Haifa apartment. Cigarette pinched between thumb and index finger, he strolls between us as we stretch our legs skyward, encouraging higher achievement by bringing the smoldering tip of his cigarette under our thighs. I am finally allowed to quit.

Ronit continues without me, still hoping to dance her way into her future. But the visa for which her family applied never arrives, the suitcase she has prepared under her bed remains empty, and I fly to America without her, leaving her to dance her way into becoming a teacher in rooms filled with little girls with big dreams.

House Cleaning

Israel

The cleaning woman is standing on the window's sill in our bathroom, screaming because the neighbor walked in and she's afraid of men. Her shrieks fill the stairwell as my mother races upstairs, where she finds the cleaning lady now hysterical, Miron, the neighbor grinning up at her, pleased to have caused such an amazing reaction. I want to climb up on the sill with the cleaning woman, see us from above, a bird's eye view. It must feel good to scream that loud at what you see below.

Silence

Israel is a noisy country. And perhaps this is why the silence in our house seems so loud. Outside our door people are never shy about making themselves heard. A neighbor yells for quiet on a summer afternoon. A teenager in the apartment across the way demands that her sister return the Jeans she borrowed without permission. A driver leans on the horn to get a slower motorist out of their way, flashing their headlights for emphasis. And in the *Shuk*, the open air market where I tag along with my grandmother, vendors shout their wares over small mountains of fragrant onions, glistening fish, sweet green grapes my grandmother piles into her plastic basket for our snack at the beach. Once there, the waves noisily crash against the shore, while young men, their muscles slick with oil play paddle-ball in the hot sand, the thwack of the small black ball part of the rhythm of the beach. Back in my grandmother's small apartment, my salty hair washed, the tar scrubbed from my feet, I lie between crisp white sheets, my sunburned legs stretched against the cool linen. Yet even here, with all the world at rest, pigeons flutter and coo on the window sill above my bed, as the drone of buses and the forlorn metal squeak of old swings in the park across the road lulls me to sleep.

But at home, despite the classical music father likes to hear on the radio each morning, and the semblance of familial bliss we try to feign, there is a heaviness of words unsaid, thoughts collected and stored in places hidden from prying eyes. Unlike the sounds around us, our noise is polite, stirring just under the surface like dry hay waiting to ignite. Father's unspoken regret for his choice of wife. Mother's disappointment at his lack of ambition for the glory she believes he can achieve and she deserves. Brother's attempts to please them both. And the clean paper before me screams Speak! While inside all of us there is turbulence, thoughts on spin cycle, a maelstrom on the horizon, in minutes threatening to touch down and once and for all, clear the air. Four tongues among us, four ways to yell, tell a joke, break a heart; whisper sweet nothings; keep appearances. Four ways to break this silence molasses thick, wet air too heavy to breathe before the storm. And yet four tongues remain silent, keeping secrets, keeping score, keeping the beat of disappointed hearts, sticking it out no matter how miserable. *Listen.* It's gathering force, going ninety in a twenty five zone, giggling in libraries, farting in public, giving the finger to cops. *Look.* It's dancing naked with the curtains open, trying to break free and say what nobody wants to hear. But the paper remains blank, a dead weight around my neck.

Treasures

Both Sides of the Sea

I'm a collector. Colorful glass marbles I spill out of a leather pouch onto my bedroom floor and sort on a dull afternoon. Stamps of exotic birds, faraway places and people father says were once important as he teaches me to soak the small bits of paper, miniature art work, in water and salt until they peel away from their envelope. In a small shoebox reside porcelain animals, each one from a tea box brought all the way from America as a gift for my grandmother, who pulls off the cellophane wrapper and lets me look for the figurine nestled among the tea bags. I once tripped on the stairs on the way up to my room sending fragile pink poodles and grayish seals skittering down the tile steps, chipping their frozen smiles beyond repair. But these are private collections, not meant for trading, like the lead creations I make with my father who shows me how to melt them down, letting them drip into water where they hiss and sizzle into frozen silvery shapes.

Then there are more common collections. Like the boxes of apricot pits, *gogos* as the local kids call them and fiercely guard as they toss them against the schoolyard walls, gambling with them during recess. The girls in my fifth grade class collect erasers, so I too, have my own handful of rubbery cats with plastic eyes shaking in their heads, bright pink erasers shaped into lips and lightly scented, and one shaped like an ice cream cone, from Orly who just wanted to be nice since there wasn't anything I had that she wanted but she gave it anyway.

There is though, a favorite collection that cannot be traded in the school yard or kept in a box under the bed. And I'm not sure my friends would understand even if I tried to explain. Why would they, since they had never been without the supply I quietly hoard and savor with each new addition. I stash away words I come across in the books that line my shelves, words that roll off my tongue when I practice saying them in secret. I watch the impact they leave on their targets' expressions, like well–aimed arrows hitting their mark. Scarlet's face crumpling with disbelief as Rhett Butler's, "Frankly my dear..." hits and explodes, not just the words themselves but the timing, a thing of beauty in its measured cadence. And the language doesn't seem to matter as I pluck the sounds out of the air when they flutter by, *parapluie* becoming mine once I taste its rainy meaning during French class one day, *limonada* sweet and sour on my tongue as Sara offers me a frosty glass of the icy drink. *Slither* snakes its way into my mental dictionary, its emerald sheen hissing around my ears. While the Arab *Salam Aleicum* is rewarded by a repetition of my own greeting, followed by a wide sweep of the shopkeeper's arm as he waves me into the colorful world of his bazaar.

The more words I collect, the stronger my voice becomes, an arsenal of sorts that allows me to speak my mind, no longer rehearsing until I get it right. This talent I perfect will one day confuse an American university official, who while reading my written answer to a placement exam, notes my place of birth and decides I must have cheated. My heavily accented mother who tends to lose her listeners the moment they hear her broken English, sends me back and forces the examiners to check again. And sure enough, I dip into my collection and under their watchful eyes I prove the sharpness of the words I've honed, earning my entry through their doors. For someone like me, always a visitor whose light accent gives her away, the power of those words and the quickness of my draw, lets people know that I belong, that I intend to stay, and that I just might have something worthwhile to say.

Running

Our street lends itself to running. From one end to the other it is one straight line, a runway allowing me to gather speed and take flight. If chased, it offers me quick hiding places, shadowy and familiar. When troubled, it stretches and yawns into the distance until my lies are perfected. Past the pitango tree, past Ashman's grocery where I am sent, painfully shy to buy a forgotten item, where I must speak the language into which I was born and cannot pronounce. Past the apartment buildings in which eyes are watching, tongues reporting, scores kept. Why do they care? I am not that interesting yet, just practicing my running. There is no need to ask where I have been. I am still predictable. School, bus stop, piano lesson, ballet; then, home by curfew. I follow the rules, never considering breaking them. Not until much later, when the pretty box we live in starts to crack and the bows I am wrapped in unravel. And once I start to spill nobody can put me back. I spill big, like those syrupy drinks you have to watch when you add the seltzer water. They hiss and fizz and up and over they go, leaving sticky red trails in their wake. I still don't know that I am soda. There is just something inside that needs to run, to be loud, to dance wildly and break all the rules. I just don't understand it yet. All I know is that running sets me free. Heart beating in my ears, the thrill of being faster than my classmates, even faster than the boys, Barak, our running coach warning to slow down or I'll use up all my energy too soon. He doesn't understand just how much speed is bottled up inside me, ready to catapult me away from my mother's elegant world. I am an explosion waiting to happen.

Botany

Israel, 1983

T he thick book on the table before me has caught my attention. Not because of its vivid cover depicting three large poppies, a dusty pink, a lipstick red and a royal purple splashing color onto each desk in the room. Not too many of my classmates are excited about the new subject being introduced, the thick botany definer our guide to the flora of Israel. But as I thumb through its pages my eyes catch a heading that makes me stop. *Natives and foreigners in the world of plants, it begins. In addition to the division of plants into wild and cultivated there is a third group of strangers…*and in that instant I believe that botany professor Michael Zahari of Jerusalem's Hebrew University is writing for me.

*On the face of the globe are areas distant from each other yet similar in their conditions for plant life. California and certain southern parts of America are very similar to Israel in climate…*how did he know that California was where we disappeared each time my mother thought we would be happier somewhere else? *It is very possible that many of these plants from other countries are capable of growing here, despite geographic obstacles in their migration, such as deserts and oceans…* from the plane's window these vast stretches of earth spread beneath me, a tapestry of terrain dangerous only if the large machine once again transporting us plummets from its unnatural height. *There is however, another obstacle, the local flora whose power is great in its competition with strangers…*I can still feel the gravelly sting of the stretch of beach where the race was about to begin. And my body bore proof of the battle we waged that morning, dressed in our running uniforms, our school's name stretched across our chests.

Dozens of girls from local schools jostled each other on the starting line, waiting for the gun to sound, for their team to win. This was not about long distance running any more. Arab girls were competing against us, and we were running for our country. I had kept going even after she tripped me, despite the bloody scrapes, the burn of tiny rocks embedded in my knees. We had won that day, sportsmanship be damned, the infection in my lacerations too much even for my mother to handle. *Even so, among the strangers can be found individuals capable of standing strong in the face of such rivalry some even gaining strength over locals until it is not easy to detect their foreignness.* My first day of third grade comes swimming into my mind's eye, the large school yard where children of all sizes yelled and chased and didn't look back once as their parents left. They eyed me curiously as they hurtled past on strong tan legs, until one skinny girl came forward, took me by the hand and plucked me away from my mother's skirt where I had been hiding. From then on I was in. *Known to all is the night candle of the beach, yet not everyone knows that this now most popular plant first infiltrated from America in the previous century.* I am *not* an infiltrator I want to tell professor Zahari, I was *born* here, just like the oxalis with its lemon yellow flowers, a weed according to the professor's definition. Would a *stranger,* an *infiltrator* know that the bright green stem is a sour treat that I, like other local children chew on our way to school? *A number of these strangers have assumed positions of power and respect alongside our shores and are here to stay, unlike others that have come and gone, disappearing as though they never existed.* We disappear once in a while; the house on Narkisim Street locked up or rented out, depending on the length of our absence. Then the wind carries me to other shores, but not for lengthy enough stays, where I walk among people I recognize but who do not register my presence. Once, in a Safeway grocery store, I saw Sherri Walker pushing a shopping cart laden with cereal and a toddler. Despite the years and weight, I recognized those beautiful eyes draped in dark lashes, the upturned nose, and I remembered how once when we were five, she threw up during nap-time, right there on her mat in Mrs. Boda's kindergarten room. But that morning in the store, so many years later, she walked right past me, with no more than a California smile, even though I still had the photo album they made me in class as a going away gift, with her drawing of an airplane flying away with me in it.

Yet here in this Israeli classroom, as I look around at the faces of classmates, these are the brothers and sisters of my childhood. My presence among them is as unsurprising as the scent of lemon blossoms perfuming the air each spring. I have learned things about them which time and distance will never erase. I know that Gilia falls asleep before anyone else at slumber parties, her red hair spilling over her pillow in a fiery cascade. I know that Yuval wants to be a rock star, refusing to cut the shock of dirty blond locks the teachers reprimand and the girl sitting behind him plays with when she's bored. And over there in the corner seat is Moshe who thinks of nothing but playing the piano, his fingers always practicing under the desk, on the back of the chair in front of him, composing symphonies only he can hear. And me; Front row center, (because mother says good students sit up front,) sharing a desk with Lee who for exams places her talismanic toy elephant between us to spread the luck. What secrets of mine do they carry in their memories? Will I disappear from the landscape of their hearts like those plants the professor writes of but does not bother to include in his guide? Those roadside weeds, neglected in the dust, out of sight in abandoned gardens. I want nothing more than to have taken root in these people's hearts, and it won't be

until many years later that I will realize I had done just that, when I will find the thin yearbook in which a teacher took the time to write to me. *You have made your mark with your quiet modesty, secretly weaving in threads of silver another lovely chapter of my life... I thought of you lately...you never spoke too much---and you inspired me to recall the words of the Little Prince: 'Only the heart can see well, because the most important thing is hidden from the eye...' And I discovered you! Be blessed and happy,*
    Miri Rom

Michal

Michal lives on the fourth floor of the apartment building on the corner of my street. Her hair is cut short like a boy's, and her small face always looks like she's about to do something adults wouldn't like. Her school uniform is too big for her small frame, and she never tucks in the pale green school shirt even though it's the rule and hanging out it looks like she isn't wearing any shorts on her long skinny legs. She loves her father because he lets her keep all the animals she finds on the way home from school. But then her sad mother throws them out and Michal asks if I want the kitten, or the turtle, or the sick pigeon she has wrapped in her coat. She found a puppy on the way to school one morning, and brought it to class. We all knew what was making that funny bulge under her sweater, but none of us told, not even the mean ones, because the puppy made her smile until she didn't even remember to cover her mouth to hide the gray tooth in front. But she couldn't keep the dog from whimpering, and the teacher finally figured it out and sent them both out into the hall.

Sometimes I see her mother walking slowly towards their apartment building, a small bag of groceries perched against her hip. I hear the gossiping housewives who sit on the low stone wall down the street, snippets of their conversations floating in our direction, "Mental hospital... depression," and then they stop when they see us kids paying too much attention. I think she's sad because she stays up on the fourth floor waiting for her soldier son to return from the army, and until he does she can't find a reason to smile. Maybe if she let Michal keep some of those animals she wouldn't be so lonely. And then her son returns one day and puts his gun to his head and shoots, right up there in his room in that fourth floor apartment. And I overhear the women on the wall saying that it was his mother who found him like that. She'd stepped out for a minute to buy bread and while she was gone he decided he'd had enough. I can't stop thinking what she must have seen when she got back and how they told Michal that her big brother was dead. And did anyone eat that bread his mother bought that day? Did anyone eat bread ever again? I don't say any of this out loud, but I'm told by my mother that I have to go pay my respects because Michal is my classmate. The very idea of going up to that apartment terrifies me. What will I say? What will I see? Will there be any tell tale signs of what he'd done? On any given day my words are tangled in my mouth like so much yarn. I don't speak in class unless spoken to, and answering when called on makes my heart beat wildly and my face turn an ugly red. Not even the pretty blush like on the cheeks of those movie actresses I see on television. But mother insists, and I walk down the street to Michal's apartment building where I push the button that turns on the stairwell light and climb to the fourth floor, running between landings so I don't get stuck on the stairs when the timer runs out and the building dips into darkness. I make it to the third floor and change my mind, racing back down and all the way to my house where I'm met by my mother's stern look before she sends me back. By the time I'm standing in front of Michal's door, my hair is damp, my face flushed, and I hope no one will hear my whisper of a knock. But the door swings open and my eyes take in a roomful of guests sitting Shiva, the customary seven days of mourning. Some faces I recognize, neighbors who came out of kindness, or curiosity at the chance to see the inside of these people's lives. I mutter something unintelligible as

I'm pointed towards Michal's room. There, gathered closely on the rug, are my classmates, talking softly, listening to an Israeli music tape; an intimate party of sorts. Michal looks up at me her eyes red, and smiles her lopsided smile that tries to hide that tooth. I learn that I don't have to say anything after all. I just need to be.

Boys

Israel

When the boy on the motorcycle comes calling for Tali, the whole neighborhood watches. That's because he rides right up the path under her bedroom window, doesn't even bother to park and walk up to the first floor apartment where she lives. He keeps the motor running like he can't be made to wait, and yells out her name, claiming her for all to hear. Her mother, Sara, leans out the kitchen window, fat breasts spilling over the sill, and yells at him, her forehead bunching up and those little eyes get smaller and meaner. "Get out of here! Leave my daughter alone!" She hollers, as neighbors' heads appear in windows for the free show, shaking from side to side and clucking in agreement with her. In the bedroom window Tali is yelling back, a lesson in daughters gone bad to those of us still obedient. My mother is watching from across the courtyard, angry that anyone would dare disturb the quiet of the afternoon. "How vulgar," she announces, not loud enough for motorcycle guy to hear over the din and roar of his machine. But I can see from his face that even if he had heard he wouldn't have cared, not someone like him, not with a smile like that. He knows he owns the world and girls like Tali, are his for the taking. Her mother may yell, but girls like Tali yell back, and do what they want. I watch her get ready for dates sometimes, standing up on the kitchen table, hot wax melting in a pot on the stove, her sister helping with the tug and pull of cloth strips up and down her legs. One pulls, one yells and I watch in awe, my insides clenching as Tali's legs begin to shine. When she isn't wearing the latest fashions she can be found bent

over a drawing pad designing them, wispy figures draped in colorful creations appearing on the blank spaces before her. I collect
these glimpses I get into the secret world of girls. No one in my
house talks of such things. No holding of hands, no early morning cuddling under the blankets. Prim and proper are the adults
in my life, and I am left to wonder about this secret subject of sex.
I greedily gather information and store it for future use, in case
someone like motorcycle guy will come for me.

Falafel

Report card days are like holidays in my house. Mother collects my brother and me from school, and sometimes a lucky friend is asked to join us to celebrate our good grades. For the span of one afternoon we are allowed to forget about homework. I don't worry about painful math lessons that I fail to understand, despite the handful of tutors who have tried to explain, including my own father. He always ends up yelling and I am left crying, incapable of following the numbers that come so easily to my brother, who claims he sees them in his dreams. "You could if you didn't keep telling yourself you can't," my mother insists, unable to accept failure of any sort. But I forget the Biblical texts we spend hours translating, recreating the lives of those who walked this land before us. I let the breeze carry away with it important dates of battles, births, meetings, *in the tent of meeting, on the first day of the second month, in the second year.* I cannot keep track of who begat whom. History, which my memory releases from its grasp the moment I am faced by the question on the blank test page I am expected to fill; And French. *Tu comprend, Elle comprend, nous comprenons. Je ne comprend pas.* Poor Monsieur Bismut, his balding head shining under the classroom's harsh fluorescent lights while trying so patiently to make me understand; and grammar. How do I explain that the only way words make sense to me is by the way their sounds sing in my ears, taste in my mouth. I picture their meaning like stories unfolding on a movie screen, not by colons, hyphens, or conjugations. No matter the language, its beauty will never speak to me through rules. My friends and I have memorized and analyzed until we can recite the information in our sleep. We will face the exam papers, say what is expected of us, please or disappoint our teachers and parents, then forget everything and begin again.

But now we are on our way to Acco, old Acre, its ramparts and minarets already beckoning from a distance as mother speeds towards the ancient city where she will reward our studiousness with an afternoon treat. I can tell we've arrived even before my mother swings into the narrow parking space, startling a small donkey as it naps in the sun. The air has taken on a salty tinge from the sea breaking against the fortified walls surrounding the old city. And as I step out onto the cobbled road it's as if I have stepped back in time. Old Arab men in *Galabias*, flowing robes, and *Kafias*, traditional headdress, sit on small stools outside store-fronts, smoking their water pipes and staring lazily at passersby. A wrinkled old woman smiles at me from her shop, where olive wood crosses and bottled holy water invite tourists to come in and leave American dollars, more precious than the *shekels* in which we deal. But we are headed towards other temptations, the local café *Abbu Christo*, where we each order falafel, and watch as the owner deftly fries the golden orbs, stuffing them into the warm pita bread. The rest is up to us. Sauces, pickled vegetables, salads, are all lined up on the counter at which we stand and create a meal fit for the men who once roamed these streets. Conquering crusaders, besieged by Saladin, the sultan of Egypt, Richard the Lion-heart, even Napoleon whose failed attempts are still evident in the canons he left behind. And as we sit in the sun, washing down our food with ice cold drinks in sparkling glass bottles, I know that under my feet is a history lesson none of my books can capture quite this way. Below city level are the Knights' Halls; intricate damp tunnels leading to a dining room, a cloister, an underground world holding secrets of our past. Surrounding these walls is a moat and medieval ramparts down which I half expect to see Templar knights charging, their white mantles flapping behind them. If I squint against the sun, I can just make out their shields, emblazoned with a red cross and two knights on one horse to demonstrate their poverty. Greek and Latin characters reveal themselves as they come closer, *Sigillum Militum Xpisti*, the seal of the soldiers of Christ. History comes alive between these walls.

My mother is speaking, repeating how proud she is that we have proven ourselves in our studies, encouraging that we persist and succeed. "Show them what kind of family you come from." By the time she is finished and I can look away without being disrespectful, I can barely make out the last of the dust kicked up by the beautiful horses of my imaginary knights, and all that is left in the narrow alley is the tired donkey, swatting at flies.

We are soon finished with the messy repast, tahini sauce on my sleeves the only evidence of what I ate. My brother is eyeing a crusader sword in the shop next door, while my friend is fingering a colorful scarf my mother will end up buying her. It is time to head back to the car, back to the lives that await us beyond this seaport's walls where it is so easy to fall short of expectations. My mother anticipates others' shortcomings and they rarely disappoint; the neighbor who interrupted her nap by yelling out the window; the Russian grocery clerk who leans against the scale and weighs her breasts along with the lemons; The man who did not rise to offer her his seat on the bus; The daughter who refused to memorize her lessons. These details my mind does not fail to remember. My mother concentrates on the road, my brother in the passenger seat beside her, while my friend and I are in the back, she admiring herself in the new scarf, and I looking out the rear window for a last glimpse of the disappearing walls of a city so many tried to breach and make their own.

Piano Lessons

My mother is convinced that I have talent. After all, I come from a long line of artists, and not having some sort of creative gift is out of the question. And because everything from obscure painters to royal photographers is on my mother's mental list of family skills, I am sent to piano lessons twice a week. These sessions take place in the empty school building after hours, when the sound of frustrated teachers and raucous students has been replaced by an unearthly stillness, broken only by my footfalls and distant music escaping from behind closed doors. I climb the three flights of steps, pausing once to gaze out onto the deserted schoolyard recuperating from the havoc of its daytime occupants. The second break in my ascent is on the third floor landing, where I stop to look at the wall size painting of the twelve tribes of Israel, chipped and fading from years of wind and irreverent hands sliding across it on their way down to the yard and freedom. *Reuven, Gad, Simeon, Levi, Benjamin, Juda...* I read their names and try to imagine a distant time and place in which I would not be on my way to piano lessons I almost dread.

Even before I push open the classroom door I can hear my classmate, Moshe showing off, our teacher Eva, leaning back in her chair, a pleased look on her usually strained face. She turns in my direction, one red lacquered finger held to her lips to indicate silence, and waves me to her side so I too, may admire the genius at work. By now Moshe has discovered my presence in the room, and his need to show me up causes his mop of hair to flop into his eyes, his tapered fingers finishing the piece with an extra flourish.

He swivels towards me, monkey grin under thick brows, all features for which he is teased during the day, when these rooms are no longer his domain. It is the after hours world that he enjoys, our own version of the hunchback swinging from his bell tower. And although I am not eager to begin my lesson, Moshe is cutting into my time so I sneer at him from behind Eva's back, even though I can tell talent when I hear it. Eva sends him on his way, and I wait for his footfalls to fade down the hall before I tackle the notes in the book before me.

The strained look has returned to Eva's face, where a slim cigarette is clasped in the lipstick slash of her mouth, her manicured hands roughly gripping mine to correct bad habits she insists, in her heavy Russian accent, were introduced by American teachers while I was away. Unlike Moshe, my music is in my heart not in my hands, and certainly not in my head, which seems to have difficulties retaining the information it takes in. This makes me unreliable when it comes to performing before an audience, since my head is busy telling my hands that they will fail, while my heart has transported me out the window of the recital hall and into the garden below where I would rather be. Not up on a stage, in an uncomfortable dress, the object of too many pairs of eyes with so many expectations. And quitting is not an option, not when mother has already attributed my knack for playing Chopin to the Polish blood the composer, like her, just happened to have flowing in his veins.

This fear of performing grows over the years, seizing me the night before a concert as I lie in bed unable to sleep. My hands held up before me, ten digits stretched at attention, I try to choose which one to damage so I will not have to play. I could let one linger in the entry and *accidentally* allow the heavy armored door to slide across my hand. Or I could help out in the kitchen where the possibilities for mishap are endless. Yet my fear of pain is even greater than my fear of playing for an audience, so I let my hands drop back to the softness of the blanket, where they and I sigh with relief at the reprieve.

By the time I am in high school and Eva has had her second nervous breakdown, I am old enough to travel by bus to a neighborhood in Haifa, where my *Savta*, my father's mother, lives with her second husband. Paul, a forgotten concert pianist whose only remaining fans are his doting wife and the handful of Hungarian immigrants who still recall his glory, waits for me in the cramped third floor apartment. Savta has seen me from the tiny balcony where she grows Geraniums, scraggly plants trailing through the rusted bars of the old neglected building. I climb the dark stairwell, damp wallpaper peeling from its walls, until out of breath I reach the landing where she awaits. No words are exchanged, since she has never learned Hebrew and I speak no Hungarian. But the warm smile in her eyes and her soap scented hands around my face speak for her. I am ushered in, where Paul in suit and tie sits waiting at the low coffee table where a sweet snack has been prepared for my arrival. From my father's few offerings of his life before the war, I know that until the Communists arrived and claimed it as their own, my grandmother once owned a sweet shop, a discovery that fills me with more delight than any of the fancy occupations my mother's side of the family can boast. On the table before me is evidence of my grandmother's sweet past, delicate pastries and a bowl of chestnut paste, a dessert I know must have taken her hours to prepare. We sit and smile at each other, my eyes traveling over walls crowded with paintings of landscapes and still life in which the dead rabbit stretched across a fruit laden table always gazes at me through its glazed eyes. Two pianos take up the little space available, one for student use only, the other for those rare occasions when Paul plays for me. His feigned reluctance at being asked to perform is short-lived, and suddenly before my eyes, an old man's face becomes young again, his aged hands lithe as they travel across the yellowed keys. I treasure these private concerts, so different from the stress-filled atmosphere of the recital halls, as well as the strained visits with my mother who tolerates her in-laws only because of the hint of past elegance the music suggests.

When it is my turn at the piano, Paul gently correcting, metronome patiently keeping beat, Savta quietly leaves the room to busy herself in the narrow kitchen where only one person at a time can fit. When it is time for me to leave, I can still feel Paul's papery dry hand patting mine, quietly repeating, "Good; good hands," almost to himself, while Savta's soapy scent lingers on my skin. I know she was listening while I played and I don't seem to mind, just as I know that Paul will remain standing in the window of the balcony, waving and watching me on the path below until I disappear around the bend.

Time's Up

I am getting used to saying goodbyes but not to the feeling of anguish that comes with them. At age eleven I hold my best friend Ronit tightly and try not to cry when she runs off before her own tears give her away. At fourteen, I run off with the dog we have to give away, my plan to hide in the nearby field until the plane carrying my family to America has left the ground. At sixteen, on the other side of the world again, an American boyfriend promises to wait for me until I come back, but his love-filled letters soon slow to a trickle, then nothing at all, until I wake up one night and can't remember the color of his eyes. And when mother decides to save me from the dangerous land I have grown to love, my father stays behind and comes to visit once a year, until his absence from the dinner table no longer hurts my lungs when I breathe and the sound of his voice on the phone is more familiar than his guest-like visits. Yet dread still fills me the night before it is time to leave, whether I am the one packing or the one watching someone else fold their life into their luggage. Suddenly the conversations take on an urgency they did not have the day before when our time together stretched out before us. I watch Ronit's face as she stands at her stove, pouring love into this meal I get to share with her once every few years. She must have made every dish she has learned to cook while I've been gone, the table covered in a tapestry of Mediterranean delights that would put any restaurant to shame. I have missed most of her early adulthood and hardly recognize the voice she uses to encourage me to eat, sounding like her mother when we were girls. I taste everything and wouldn't dream of refusing seconds; after all, this may very well be our last meal together. In his garden later that evening, I watch my father's hands wielding old pruning shears as he does battle with his roses, and I try to memorize the shape of his fingers before I fly away from him again. We stay up late into the night, giving up sleep we desperately need before another long journey away from people who are like body parts we'll miss, our hearts still reaching for them like phantom pains of limbs lost. So much to say and so few hours left, our deadline approaching like an executioner's footfalls down a death row corridor. Conversations that could fill a lifetime are condensed into allotted portions, real time translated into narrative time, but my story is too long to tell in one night, Scheherazade postponing a fast approaching end.

Life Lines

October 11, 1979

Thanks for the nice letter! I'm so excited that you're coming back so soon! You'll be right around the corner from me. We've started school here too. I'm going to the new Emerson they built out in Westwood. We go to school from 9:15 – 2:30, can you believe it!? Remember how I used to have a fake corner on my front tooth? I just got that capped (ouch). How long will you stay in the U.S. this time? Hope it's longer than last time!

Your friend always,
Karen

May 19, 1982

How are you? Everything's all right here except I'm stressed from all the government exams I'm taking. But I found time to write to you. I go out almost every Friday with guys a year older than us, and last week I celebrated my birthday with them. You should see the crazy clothes they're wearing in Israel now -Pants that reach just below the knee, in wild colors, like pink and purple and red. I bought myself a pair and sewed one, too. Well, that's all. I'm already looking forward to your return.

Your friend who misses you,
Ronit

June 10, 1983

Well, Gee Chick! Do you miss the good ol' U.S.? We miss you!! It must feel weird to be in a different country after being here for so long. Did you have to readjust? I'm in a show right now. It's called

Carnival. It's about a French girl who joins a traveling carnival and talks and sings with the puppets. I'm a carnie. Actually I'm one of the dance hall girls, fishnet stockings and all. Boy do I miss you. There is a girl at my school named Lara and she reminds me of you sometimes. She's from Iraq and she speaks in the same sort of precise English that you do. Do you speak in English at home? Did you get your dog back? Do you miss me? I'll write you again for sure.

Good-bye with lots of love,
Maggie

September 21, 1983

I received your letter today. It took 11 days to get here. Have you got my letters? The night we said good-bye was terrible. I kept thinking that I wouldn't see you any more after that night. I hope it gets easier, I think about you all the time. I don't ever want to go through a night like that again, ever. I wish I could talk with you. Maybe if I yelled really loud? Please write back, and write long letters.

I love you,
David

February 14, 1984

Happy Valentine's Day! How are you doing? I received your letter last week. I'm sorry I haven't written either. I have been very busy. I was admitted to U.C.D, I can hardly believe it! I can't wait to see you again; only five more months. You are coming back, aren't you?

Love,
David

Welcome home! I hope you're not too tired and that you had a good trip. It's strange that you'll be reading this at home, and not in America. I won't be back from the base until Friday, and you will have been home for a whole week without my being able to come see you! I'll come straight from the station in my uniform, and I have so much to tell you. Be prepared for many hours of gossip and don't you dare not be there when I arrive!

Missing you terribly,
Lee

This Never Happens in my House

I didn't mean to stare, I'd been taught not to, but on my way to the bathroom in Tali's apartment I pass the open door to the room she will share with her sister until her wedding day. Tali is seated on a chair facing the door, her boyfriend brushing her hair as he stands behind her. Her thick mane is clutched in one of his hands while the other gently runs the brush through light brown strands, a look of contentment on his lean face. *This is what I want*, I think to myself, unable to explain the yearning I feel at this simple picture of a man brushing his future wife's hair. I stand and watch this scene I translate as love, until she looks up and waves, her eyes smiling, happy to share this private moment with me. I know I don't live like other teenage girls. I don't have their easy ways and lightning tongues. Their effortless give and take with boys they choose to date. They speak up in class without their ears burning hot; they call out to the bus driver if he's missed their stop. They wear the latest fashions, tight fitting skirts that hug their hips, shirts with sleeves that drop precariously off shoulders. My mother's puritanical ways keep me in modest and childlike clothes, and her heavy hand through my untamable hair is accompanied by one of her favorite sayings. "For beauty one must suffer," she announces as I yelp when the brush hits a snag.

Those other girls loudly declare their presence in this world, their confidence a shimmering radiance I can see while I remain moored, incapable of untying the marionette strings that keep me just within my mother's reach. I have seen the world's beauty as we travel from shore to shore, life to life like restless hummingbirds never touching down. I've lain on the marble floors of the Sistine chapel; Michelangelo's ceiling filling my eyes with beauty. I've stood at the edge of the Grand Canyon, watching a hawk suspended over the yawning maw of nature, sapphire sky and feathery clouds under its outstretched wings. But all I want is the easy grace with which these girls walk down a city street, the assurance with which they ask a vendor for a cold drink, *orangada* please, then the careless way they wipe the soda's fizz from their glossy lips. All I want is a boy in my room brushing my hair.

Hair

California, 1981

I don't give much if any thought to my legs and their fine covering of dark hair until I am in the ninth grade in a California junior high school. Hovering between countries means we are forever novelties, set apart by our foreignness. And while this makes me somewhat an object of interest, it also means I am forever missing pieces of information that could help me fit into the crowd. Like joining a game after the rules have been explained and the players for each team picked. So when a boy named Kurt points at me during lunch recess one afternoon and yells "Look at her hairy knees!" A wave of shame washes over me as I try to hide these displeasing parts of my body I didn't know I had until that moment. Not only am I unfamiliar with the American obsession with smooth, hairless bodies I also have a mother who forbids me to change anything with which I was born. I am allowed no make up unless I am in a stage performance. "Only cheap women wear paint on their faces. Besides," my mother persists. "You are beautiful as you are." She cannot understand these American mothers who allow their daughters to walk out of the house with so much *war paint*, as she calls it. When my first day of American junior high arrives, she brings me to school and marvels at the parade of girls walking by, make up, calf length dresses and high heels clicking past us down the corridors. I am in awe of their beauty, their natural grace and ease as they giggle with their heads together, sharing secrets. My mother stares in disbelief, whispering loudly that had they been *her* daughters, she'd drag them into the bathroom and wash off all that *war paint*. The subject of shaving is cut short when I dare suggest she allow me to remove underarm hair. "Never!" she warns; eyes wide as if I've just mentioned the other taboo subject in our house, sex; "Never! It will grow back thicker and darker." I don't dare to ask again. But today the end of the school day cannot arrive fast enough, and I pedal home furiously, relieved to find the house empty as I set out to remove the offensive hair. My father is across the seas, my brother too young to shave, so there are no razors in the house. I set to work with a small pair of sharp nail scissors, while seated on a chair by the window for better light. One by one, I cut the dark hairs anywhere I can reach; my hands quick and determined in the short span of time I know I have before my mother's return. By the time she steps in, I have put away the scissors and there is an odd gleam in my eye and on my naked legs. I feel strangely victorious.

*   *   *

California, 1982

I begin tenth grade as a Blue Devil, its horned and bearded face leering from the walls of the California high school I will attend for one year before returning to Israel. Back home mascots are unheard of, the only distinguishing feature between schools the color of our uniforms. So far our travels to America have allowed me to be an owl and an eagle and I'm not sure what the switch from animal to diabolical portends. It is along these halls that I see the American teenage caste system come to life, all represented in caricature like vividness as I walk from class to class. Cheerleaders in tiny ruffled skirts and perfect hair stand giggling at anyone passing by who is not one of them. Athletes in baseball caps and tight jeans stride confidently past cheerleaders who smile and simper. In the far corner gather Mexican students, the boys in wide black pants and white sleeveless undershirts, their dark good looks reminding me of home. The girls' eyes send daggers towards the cheerleaders, thick lipstick sneers curling their mouths. Coming from a school system that cast us all in the same nondescript uniform, I find this division both telling and entertaining at the same time.

I soon fall into a strange little group of my own, my participation in the school's choir introducing me to an artistic set of students who happily welcome me into their midst. One girl in particular takes me under her wing, Maggie, whose wide set green eyes contain a perpetual look of mischief I find intriguing if somewhat alarming. Unlike me, who prefers not to call attention to myself, Maggie declares her presence with her whole being; from the grin that stretches across her impish face to the strange choice of clothes she throws together, bangles jangling, earrings clicking, her heavy sweet perfume wafting down hallways in her wake. One afternoon she bursts into the music room and in a stage whisper asks, "Guess what I'm not anymore?" I feel foolish when the other girls seem to understand while I still wait for an explanation. Seeing my confusion Maggie leans over, eyes shining, and with her hot breath in my ear whispers, "A virgin silly!" I can't think of anything else for the rest of the day, my eyes wandering in her direction all through rehearsal to see if she looks any different. She is radiant. I want to know if it was Robert she did it with, an older boy whose two younger half-brothers I babysit even when he's home because their mother doesn't trust him, but I am too embarrassed to ask. When James, a boy I have been eyeing asks me out on a date, boy crazy Maggie invites me to her home to prepare for this momentous occasion, insisting that I borrow a pair of her shoes as she glances at my unassuming footwear in dismay.

"We can do better than that," she declares. "I have just the thing." And since she clearly knows more about men than I do, I agree to try them on.

Once we arrive at her home I quickly forget the purpose of my visit. I am too busy trying not to gape at the messiest house I have ever seen. The kitchen counters are covered in unwashed dishes, mismatched furniture clutters the living room, and a small woman with short dark hair yells hello from an armchair where she sits barefoot and cross-legged, watching a television show I can't see from where I stand. I wave back as Maggie drags me towards her bedroom where the floor is lost under mounds of clothing she must have simply removed and dropped right where she stood. The sickly sweet scent of her perfume hangs over her room like an invisible fog, mingled with the stale smell of unwashed laundry. From somewhere deep within this mess sounds the muffled ringing of a phone, and after a hurried attempt to find the cord, Maggie gives up and goes in search of the shoes instead.

"Found them!" She straightens up, triumphantly dangling a pair of shoes the likes of which I would never consider buying, let alone wearing out where people might see me. They glitter in the dim light of her bedside lamp, purple sequins freckling rounded toes and covering the small heels she has cupped in her hands, her arms outstretched, waiting for me to take them. I don't know how to respond without offending and I reach out, a half-hearted gurgle of appreciation in my throat. My mother would have a fit if she saw me in these.

"Try them on! These are my lucky shoes." Maggie steps over her clothes and pushes me towards the bathroom where I can prepare for the date I am certain to frighten away in these purple creations. As I stand before the mirror wishing I looked more like American high school girls, the door I haven't bothered to lock is pushed open and there stands Maggie's mother, her wide smile reminiscent of her daughter's.

"Hi, I'm Lynn. Maggie's told me all about you. You're from Israel?" I nod as she steps into the bathroom, walks over to the toilet and prepares to pee. I mutter something unintelligible as I back towards the door, unsure how to react.

"Oh don't leave on my account. You can talk to me while I pee." I turn towards the mirror, fussing with a curl to avoid looking, while Lynn continues prattling on as if relieving herself in front of her daughter's friends is an every day occurrence. Despite my newness in this country, I'm pretty certain this isn't typical American behavior, and I smother a giggle as I picture any of the mothers of my Israeli friends doing the same. But then I cannot imagine any of them living in such messy conditions, their apartments always gleaming as though guests might walk in at any given moment. Lynn flushes the toilet as she tells me she is Bahai, and dreams of visiting Israel one day so she can see the Golden Dome. I politely extend an invitation as I make a note to myself to be sure to lock bathroom doors if she ever follows through with her plan and takes me up on the offer.

"Those look great on you!" Maggie squeals her approval when she sees me wobbling down the hall, and I don't have the heart to tell her that I don't feel like me with these things strapped to my feet. I lack the kind of confidence needed to deal with the attention wearing such shoes will attract, and I'm nervous enough about going out on my first date with an American boy since our arrival in this country.

I need not have worried. After introducing me to her mascara and lip-gloss, Maggie sees me off to the movies where James is already waiting for me. His eyes never leave my face as we walk into the theater, and once the lights dim he is too busy trying to muster up the courage to hold my hand to bother noticing what's on my feet. For nearly two hours I sit with my hand clasped in his sweaty grip and after the movie we walk down to the local ice cream parlor, where James still holds my hand over chocolate sundaes. I start enjoying the attention of this tall American boy whose heart I have captured even though I will be leaving him in a year's time when we return to Israel. But tonight, I am an American teenager in purple sequin shoes, and I feel very lucky.

Gili

I am replanted in Israeli soil at age sixteen, and when he holds my hand for the first time, all I can compare him to is the clammy handed boy I said goodbye to on a distant shore. But this one is not a boy, and his large warm hand takes mine without asking, presumptuous, enticing. I look into dark laughing eyes and almost drown in the desire I see but do not yet understand. There in the schoolyard I am chosen. My friends shrink into the background, whispering warnings against those eyes. I blush, basking in the attention of this schoolyard god. I have just returned to my old school after spending two years among polite American teenagers. I don't know this young man's reputation and his grip around my small hand is all I need as an introduction. Mother will not approve of his forward nature, his groping hands and booming laugh. I will be his to spite her, to revel in all that is forbidden in my house, to belong. I am drawn to his lack of self-consciousness, his ability to say and do what he pleases when it suits him. He is known to all and in a matter of days so am I because I'm Gili's girl. He enjoys a freedom I have yet to learn, coming from a world in which my every move is censored, accounted for, proper. I let him pull me into the empty classroom at the furthest end of the school, where I breathe in the soapy scent of his neck as he draws me into his lap, there on the cement floor. Those confident, warm hands travel over my skin as I burrow into the folds of his heavy winter coat. There I discover the beauty of his anatomy, allow my fingers to trace warm muscles until I reach the isthmus of his neck and alight there, amazed at the light fluttering I feel in that small bowl under my fingers. I am safe, convinced that he would save me from any threat, until the strings my mother pulls from afar snap taut, ending my geography lesson and sending me out of his embrace and back into the schoolyard, distant thunder mingling with his laughter. He tries once more, this time against the thick walls of the bomb shelter behind our house; now I am protected twofold, until one of the neighbors tells my mother, and I am forbidden from seeing him again.

But I am addicted, to his large hands in which mine disappear, to the crinkling of his eyes the moment I appear, to his easy ways which make me feel wanted, necessary. Disobeying, I run through dusk gathering streets to meet him at the edge of darkening fields of bleeding cockscombs velvety to the touch. Beautiful hands eagerly explore me as my eyes take in sky and I breathe in the damp sweetness of the field beneath my back, a new feeling of wildness born under my ribs. His throaty voice mingles with the evening song of crickets, and as my hand is led into unfamiliar regions, the world I come from screams in my ears and I am on my feet, startling crickets into silence. His laugh dies in his throat, his dark eyes plead as I escape, back to the familiar world my mother has created and in which I belong but do not. He gives chase down the boulevard, still intrigued enough by my foreignness to spend some energy on pursuit. But I'm too quick, too well behaved, too naïve to realize he has much more to teach. I am running in the wrong direction.

Kobi

Israel, 1983

I can't remember what you said that made me feel beautiful. Maybe because you were beautiful too, there under the olive trees, our classmates busy with teenage gossip. You were everything the men I came from were not. A face chiseled by sun, shoulders thick with muscle, hands that could protect or break a neck, depending on the circumstance. I volunteered information, Red Riding Hood inviting wolf, *Come devour please.* You came, silently watching, discovering primness seeping from my pores. *This one listens to mama,* your eyes said, *no straying off the path here* and you were gone. Until you fell out of the sky and remembered me. "I'm hurt," is all I needed to hear. Two buses and an underground to your hospital bed, a basket of goodies on my arm, past wounded soldiers, trying not to look at their injuries but looking anyway, not knowing what I'd find missing from your perfect form. There you were; dark against white sheets, sheepish grin on your wolf face, a girl the color of cocoa perched on the edge of your bed. You were right after all. I am too polite. I nod hello, smile at your girl, and leave you with my basket to explain.

Desert Stranger

Judean Desert, Israel, June 1984

I had noticed them eyeing us from their side of the camp, curiosity and suspicion mingling on their faces. Our singing was drawing them near, our voices rising as flames from the campfire leaped towards the night sky. Clearly we were not the only ones brought to the Judean desert for our senior trip, the adventure we had been mindful of each year when the senior class gathered under our classroom windows, packing the buses with their luggage and excitement. This morning had been our turn, as younger students crowded around the upper story windows, their history and geography lessons forgotten as they watched us disappear past the school's gates.

He must have been a counselor, the set of his shoulders and the calmness in his stance setting him apart from the frenzied behavior of the teenagers around him. "They're *Arabs*," friends warned, noticing my curiosity, maintaining their distance, their singing a challenge to a friendly battle on this desert night. I hadn't made their observation and only now detected the Arab words being flung in song across the campfire, a popular Israeli song thrown back. But I was not interested in singing or competing, our differences temporarily forgotten, as I stood mesmerized by the beauty and savageness of this stranger's face. I turned away from the flames, my heated face feeling the coolness of the night air, and taking a few steps away from the crowd was surprised to see the subject of my interest before me. He had stepped out of the dark as if carved from it, a jagged scar from cheek-bone to jowl perceptible now that he was close. "Are you with that group?" He lifted his chin, indicating my classmates behind us. "Yes, we arrived this afternoon." There was no harm in exchanging pleasantries, and I could always slip back into the safety of the crowd if I needed to. "Would you like to walk?" I could now detect his faint accent, the sound both familiar and dangerous at the same time. His eyes were dark but kind, unsettling yet inviting. I shoved the voice I was supposed to listen to out of the way, hearing only the other, the siren call that drew me towards the forbidden, and against my better judgment and my classmates' nervous giggling, I nodded yes.

The desert wasn't new to me. My family had headed this way on several occasions, camping down the road on the shore of the Dead Sea. I loved coming here as a child despite my mother's rigorous forays into the desert, my pale skinned brother blistering in the unforgiving sun, her dutiful daughter following her at breakneck pace over the rocky terrain. Our trips were organized, purposeful, no time wasted in my mother's need to see it all, to make good use of our stay. Even canvas and sand hadn't prevented her from maintaining domestic propriety, asking that my father surround our tent with rocks, a perimeter indicating borders not to be crossed and evoking hilarity in other campers. Our drive down from Jerusalem into the Judean Desert was uneventful, despite my mother's precautions as we passed bombed out buildings, remnants of Arab homes razed to the ground as punishment for terrorist acts. "Put your head in your pillow until I tell you it's safe," she would order, anticipating an attack from some source invisible to my eyes as I dared a quick peek out the car window.

And now here I was, deliberately separated from the crowd, walking into the wild remoteness of this ancient land with a complete stranger, not even a pillow for protection.

"Can you hear the sea murmuring?" He was asking, and for

a moment all I could hear were the now distant strains of singing carried on the gathering wind, a primitive sound followed by someone keeping beat on the back of a makeshift drum. A few more steps and this terrain over which so many battles had been fought would be under Jordanian rule. If I stayed where I stood I would be under Israeli control. Yet if I yelled, neither side would hear me. Perhaps my voice would rise on that wind and reach the caves we had passed earlier in the day, Bedouin shepherds briefly looking up at the intrusion. And then there it was. The gentle lapping the stranger had heard long before I paid it attention. He strode on ahead lighting the way with the heavy flashlight in his hand, his steps confident. I caught up, joining him where he stood on the shore of the Dead Sea, a silvery moon suspended and casting its shimmering light on the salty expanse gently rocking before us.

"What you are hearing are the laments of the dead." He paused, waiting for recognition. I listened, not trusting my voice not to give away the slight fear I now felt. "You must know the story of Sodom and Gomorra?" I nodded. He went on. "The tale goes that the sites of these ancient and wicked cities are believed to lie beneath this sea, which explains why no life forms can survive the saltiness of their useless tears." So it wasn't magnesium or calcium chloride like the science teacher had explained. This I kept to myself, liking the version I had just learned better.

"You must be tired. We should head back before you're missed." Until he had said it I hadn't realized just how tired I was, the early morning and long bus ride catching up to me now.

"Our counselors would never know the difference," I answered, noticing the mistake of my admission too late.

"Irresponsible aren't they?" I nodded, impressed that he had so quickly assessed the relaxed nature of our chaperones, and we turned away from the sinners' laments. By the time we arrived back to camp only a handful of stragglers remained sitting around the glowing embers of the fire, poking sticks at forgotten potatoes we had roasted for our suppers. A couple embraced, hidden by the now weakened light of the flames. Aside from a few hushed conversations a deep silence had fallen over the camp as my escort, one gloved hand cupped under my elbow, helped me over tent lines and stakes, wished me a good night, and walked back into the darkness from which he had come.

"Where have you been?" My tent mate, Ronit, sat up in her sleeping bag, gripping the flashlight I knew she must have left on during my absence.

"Walking." I didn't want to explain that of which she would not approve.

"Alone?" I knew that the horror in her voice would only grow once I told her about my companion. "Of course not alone. I went with someone from the other camp." "The Pirate?" So that was what they were calling him. News traveled fast. I could hear the accusation in her voice.

"Actually, he was very nice. Now go to sleep."

"Everyone's talking about you."

"Let them."

*   *   *

The earlier news report had been accurate, and when the storm hit it did so with a ferociousness of ironically biblical proportions. Wind howled and whipped our tent flaps into a frenzy followed by the crash of the camp's generator into our midst. Ronit shrieked and ran for cover while I made for the counselors' tent for help. Yelling to make myself heard over the gale, I stood waiting until a bleary eyed head poked out of the opening. "What do you need?" He yawned, squinting against the rain. "The generator fell into our tent! We need help to set it back up!" I could feel the water running down my back, dripping from my hair, into my sleeves, down into my socks. "Sleep in someone else's tent, we'll fix it in the morning…" the head was retreating into the tent and I grabbed the flap, tried again. "The report said flashfloods, we can't stay!" Thunder rumbled in the distance, lending emphasis to my words. But he didn't care. "You're old enough to figure it out. See you in the morning." And he was gone, back into the comfort of his dry sleeping bag.

Tripping through puddles I made my way back to what was left of our tent, hoping to salvage anything that may have remained dry. The large suitcase my mother had filled with food sat unharmed, while the rest of our belongings were a soggy mess. I didn't know where Ronit had gone, and I was too shy to invite myself into my classmates' tents. I wanted to sit on my suitcase and cry, weep my helplessness into the storm until someone would hear me and come make this all better. I was just considering the low building that housed the bathrooms as my shelter for the night when in the distance swung a small light, a single eye approaching and growing brighter, the rain illuminated in silvery strands against its beam; A flashlight, grasped in the gloved hand of the stranger who had once again crossed over to our side unexpectedly. "Need help?" He was pulling at ropes, adjusting stakes even before I had a chance to answer, pushing the fallen generator aside and creating a dry nest as if fishing wet girls out of desert storms was a regular habit.

"This is the best we can do for now. You can sleep." He gestured in invitation and I stepped in, relieved to be out of the rain but also soaked to my skin. I needed to change, but I couldn't throw my rescuer back into the storm. He understood. "I'll watch the entrance while you find some dry clothes." He turned and squatted at the tent's mouth, leaning back on his heels and filling the entrance with his broad shoulders. I reached for the suitcase, hurriedly peeling off the drenched clothes and replacing them with the first items my hands found in the dark, enjoying the feel of dry cloth against my skin. "Thank you. I don't know what I would have done without your help." He turned, dark eyes taking me in. "You're not like the others in your group." He wasn't asking, merely making an observation. "No, we don't seem to have much in common," I answered, all too aware of the distance my frequent absences from this country had created.

"Good. Do you have anything to eat?" I pointed towards the suitcase. "It's all yours, enjoy." Unzipping the case he whistled softly, taking in the pita bread, the salami, and the bell peppers my mother had packed the day before. "How long were you staying here?" It was the first time I had seen him smile, the scar briefly disappearing, taking most of the wildness in his face away with it.

The rest of the night was spent eating, talking, and enjoying the unexpected ease we felt in each other's company. While the storm raged we were safe, my protector and I; screened from a world that was sure to misunderstand. I don't know when I fell asleep, but I knew that he was there, just as certain of his absence the next morning when muted light seeped into the tent along with the scent of brewing coffee. Inexplicable sadness filled me as I stepped into the cool morning air, the desert giving no indication of the storm it had battled with during the night. No trace of wind other than a gentle breeze swaying the tops of palms; and no sign of the opposite camp ever having dotted the landscape with their colorful tents, their version of the night's sounds, or the kindness of which I now knew they were capable.

Soldiers

Israel, October 1984

Within moments of being deposited by the bus, we are in a line having uniforms thrust into our arms, boots, eating utensils, Uzis and kitbags out of which we will be living for the next three weeks. All of us seem to be wearing the same dazed look, unsure how to react in these strange surroundings. I wish desperately that Ronit were here by my side, but her draft notice came before mine and I watched her head towards her own adventure alone. She hadn't said goodbye, simply turning her back on me and climbing the steps into the bus, my heart breaking at her callousness, not understanding that she didn't want me or the other girls to see her cry. About to turn away I was just in time to see her hand waving at me through the narrow opening in her window. I hoped they knew that she threw up on buses if there wasn't enough air.

Now the line has led us into a room where like so many cattle we are being immunized, asked to offer our left arm, then a cheek. I'm having trouble with my pants, and when the burly soldier sees that I've got shorts under my sweats, (my mother's idea), a deep chuckle starts somewhere in his gut and bursts out in a loud guffaw. "You got a lock on there, too?" And just like that, my shyness is gone as I laugh along with him before my ass feels the bite of the syringe in his hand. The word ass tastes good in my mouth, now that I am no longer in my mother's salon, what Israelis call their living rooms. Later that night, lying on a cot in a tent with nine other girls, my muscles throb from the shots and the stress as I listen to the plaintive whimpering of the American girl in the last cot across the way. Unlike me she can't disguise her other home, and she clearly does not belong. Her weight slows her down as we run and causes her cot to collapse in the dead of night, the rest of us scrambling to see if any damage has been done to her gun, which like ours is locked to the end of her bed. She needs to boil her contact lenses, she needs special lotions for her chapped hands, *she needs to go home,* I think to myself, her attempt at being Israeli clearly backfiring. On the other hand, I need to prove that I fit in. I ask the last girl on guard duty each night to wake me an hour before we have to rise. In the velvety dark I walk across the dusty camp towards the low building looming ahead, my clean uniform already rolled in the towel under my arm so that after I wash I can wear it under my sweats to save time. Under dim lights I step into cement stalls, better that I not see what I am stepping on in there under the cold shower. By the time tired girls wipe sleep from their eyes, I am washed, dressed and smoothing out the wrinkles on my blankets before inspection. My gun is shined within an inch of its life and our runs through surrounding orange orchards a familiar task in this game I have entered. Like my mother's etiquette, not all the army's rules make sense but I learn to work with them to survive. I want to be treated like everyone else and here my family's name doesn't mean a thing.

Misplaced

I had been missing for a handful of hours, an experience I would learn to perfect even though this first time was not deliberately my doing. Three weeks of boot camp came to an end, all of us loaded into buses, grasping slips of paper with our new assignments. The day had been spent deciding fates, and I was awfully close to being claimed by the military police, until they read my paperwork and got to the part about my bad back. It was the first time since my military adventure began that I had allowed this weakness to play in my favor. "Fool," the other girls teased on that very first day, when I was told I didn't have to run with a full pack and my gun and did anyway. I kept quiet, not knowing how to explain that I just wanted to be like everyone else. Not the professor's daughter, not the American, not the new girl. And I liked to run, the oranges in the trees a sweet blur as I raced past them. Yet everyone knew what sort of person joined the military police, the kind that couldn't keep secrets and told on you behind your back. The kid who reminded teachers they forgot to assign homework. I didn't want to be one of those. Luckily they didn't want me either, as I stood before their make-shift recruitment table, slumping a bit for effect, years of being reprimanded about my posture ruined in an instant.

Girls had been dispersed in all directions of our small country, temporarily freed birds in army green, soon to be replaced by the khaki of the air force or the blue of navy uniforms, depending on their placement. Most recruits welcomed the chance to spread their wings, flying as far as the furthest border or the army's need would allow. On the other hand I was like a homing pigeon, being considered for the base down the road from our house, not thirty minutes away from my mother's still watchful eye. And being close to home meant being close to Sasha, the boyfriend for whom I'd made the less than patriotic move back to Israel, despite my acceptance to the university in California where my father taught. Sasha was a Russian immigrant; a violinist I rehearsed with at the music conservatory whenever the music he was performing required piano accompaniment. I had tried to ignore the sidelong glances he sent over the bridge of his violin, unusually long lashes veiling surprisingly blue eyes. But he could make his violin sing, and I believed that anyone who could make music like that come out of a piece of wood was worthy of my attentions. After walking me home a handful of times, I agreed to go out with him, giving him my phone number which he scribbled in chalk on the case of his violin. I told myself I was being benevolent to a newcomer in my country. My mother encouraged me to be kind to him as well, never anticipating the hold he would soon have over me and recalling her own immigrant experience all too vividly.

The base I had requested happened to be of highest security, which is why I was now on a bus heading towards an unknown destination to determine whether I could be trusted in a place where keeping secrets was a prerequisite for the job. I was doing well so far, since no one I knew had any idea where I'd gone, including me.

After several phone calls to various authorities, my mother resigned to waiting until I returned. She was told that I was probably out having fun, "You know how girls that age are," one police officer laughingly assured her, unaware of the insult to my proper upbringing. Having dealt with his share of overprotective parents, another official condescendingly announced "Don't worry, she's ours now, mommy," not knowing that she hadn't relinquished the reins just yet. *Her* daughter checked in before making any decisions on her own, and certainly didn't go gallivanting without her knowledge. And even though I wasn't doing anything questionable while off her radar, I was discovering that with the end of basic training had come the end of my shyness. For three weeks I had undressed, showered, and slept in close proximity to complete strangers. Entire nights were spent guarding dark orchards, weapon in hand, with one other girl we had learned to trust with our nightly fears. Slow, suffocating moments passed crouched under tarps, inhaling the rubbery stink of gas masks, preparing for chemical warfare, our minds replaying the training film with the dog writhing in agony from the gas's effects. And now, I found myself speaking to complete strangers on the bus. Working mothers on their way home to work some more, soldiers, heading towards a quick taste of their mothers' cooking before returning to the base; And a new me. Answering questions, sharing stories, my recent assignment arranged and a temporary base chosen until my security cleared. No information to keep confidential yet, and a few hours of anonymity until the bus would reach my station and again, I would have to be me. My mother once said "You don't have to tell people everything about yourself, learn to ask questions and listen." But now I spoke freely, gestured creatively, and enjoyed the easy banter I had grown accustomed to in the last month. Thrown so closely together with other girls my age, without parental supervision, I didn't notice that I had picked up other people's habits and dropped some of my own. There was an aggressiveness I now wore as if the army had issued it to me along with my ill-fitting uniform, and the eating utensils we were warned against losing. Within moments of receiving the tin cup and silverware I was missing a fork, having set them all down to adjust a loose boot lace. The sergeant's warning still ringing in my ears, I had turned around and taken the fork of the girl sitting next to me, quickly learning the rules of the new world to which I now belonged. If we weren't fast enough, food would be gone, so a quick pace and a smile at the cook went a long way. That smile must have been a winner, since on the day I first tried it, the cook asked me if I'd like a fresh lemon, tossed the fragrant fruit for me to catch, then told me to come stand next to him while the other girls did the dishes. All ten girls in a tent had to show up to roll call at the same time, having agreed on what to wear. If one of us wanted socks with sandals while the rest wore boots, we had to convince the misguided individual to conform, how to do so was left up to us. I was not aware of these changes in my demeanor until my mother pointed them out, her dismay evident on her face as she carefully watched this stranger who had moved into her daughter's body.

Yet the transformation was only temporary. After a few days of mimicking the hand gestures of the girl that had bunked to my right, and another few days of speaking with a throaty Sephardic lilt in my voice, the unwelcome guests bowed off the stage I had become. Soon after, my security cleared and I was introduced to the base that would become my daytime home for the next two years. I wore a green uniform each morning, showed my identification at the heavily guarded gate, said goodbye to the other girls in the unit and made my way down the long dirt road that led to the most tightly secured building on the base. Nothing I saw or heard could be repeated, not to the other soldiers in my unit, not to friends who asked what I did all day, not to my mother to whom I returned home promptly on the evening bus. Everything I now did I kept to myself.

*   *   *

Before my security clears and I am allowed to enter the highly guarded unit in which the next two years will be spent, the army temporarily places me in a Haifa base to wait it out. I spend the first few days doing odds and ends such as making small mountains of sandwiches for a group of soldiers going out in the field, folding parachutes, my hands shaking with the thought of what could happen if I didn't get it right. A few days after my arrival, I am told that I must stay the next night since the base is never left unattended and they need all soldiers, even temporaries like me, to participate in the shift rotation. Unlike others who walk away grumbling about the inconvenience, I feel a quick thrill in my gut for the rare opportunity this obligation has just afforded me. Staying at the base means not going home, where what good girls are forbidden to do is still made very clear by my mother. A good girl did not wear makeup, did not talk back to her mother, and always sat with her legs crossed to prevent men from getting the wrong ideas. A good girl did not have such ideas to begin with, certainly not the kind that involved sleeping with her boyfriend, which would cause everyone to talk and bring shame on the family. I call Sasha with the good news before I even leave the base that night, knowing that I would not have enough privacy for such a conversation at home where the walls have eyes and ears. The plan is to wait until the last roll call of the evening, then sneak him in through the hole in the fence once it is dark. Even a novice like me knows that every base has its hole and I explain to Sasha where this one is. My bus ride that night is spent daydreaming, and I can't wait to share my secret with Ronit whose apartment I quickly visit before I return home.

"If your mother finds out she'll kill you." Not the reaction I had hoped for.

"Then let's make sure she doesn't find out." I should have

told Lee who would have shrieked in delight and given me some advice.

*　　*　　*

The next day crawls by, the various tasks I am asked to fulfill barely keeping my mind from wandering towards the evening. When the last roll call takes place and everyone is accounted for, I say my goodnights and head for my quarters, a long wooden shack to the right of the main gate. I sit on the narrow cot with its thin, scratchy army issue blanket, my nerves on edge with every sound I hear until a slight knock at the bolted door makes me jump to my feet. Sasha flashes me a quick smile before I drag him inside and lock the door behind him. He sweeps me into his arms in a tight grip as I breathe in the leather of his jacket mingled with the smoke from his cigarettes. Within moments we are on the cot, overwhelmed with desire and the incredible good fortune of such rare privacy. Our dates so far, when not surrounded by Sasha's group of friends, have consisted of hurried groping on park benches, dark stairwells and sandy beaches, the chance of being discovered always weighing heavily on my mind. I had been unwilling to do anything more than kiss as his hands trailed up and down my shirt, eager but restrained. Tonight promised to be different.

"Take off your uniform." His voice is a hoarse whisper somewhere in the region of my neck.

"What if someone hears us?" Even as I say it I know it isn't possible, the main building clearly out of ear shot. My mind is teeming with good girl mantras, my mother's voice rattling them off as if she was right there in the room watching, lips held in a thin disapproving line. I shake my head loose of her voice and let myself fall into Sasha's body, his breath coming quick as he helps me struggle out of my protective greenery. Along with my clothes, the world is falling away from me, the base, the indefinite wait for the next assignment, my mother's house with all its rules, slipping off me as I give myself up to this blue-eyed musician who so clearly wants *me*. His desire gives me a sense of power and purpose, a glimpse into myself as a being with ability to affect others. Nothing else I have ever done has given me this new feeling of control, the immediate result of my behavior registering in the huskiness of his voice, in the brightness of his eyes, in the very cadence of his quickened pulse. I savor this discovery until a loud knock on the wooden door makes us both freeze, as I become aware of the wool blanket's scratchiness against my bare skin and the cool turn the night air has taken. The knock is repeated, impatient and followed by a yelled command.

"Drill! Open the door! It's a drill!" I scramble off the cot, trailing blanket and random bits of clothing behind me as I run to the door to acknowledge the deep male voice.

"I'll be right there! I just have to get dressed!"

"Hurry up! The lieutenant is waiting." I hold my breath and wait until I hear the messenger's steps grow fainter. Turning towards the room, I see Sasha leaning back against the pillow, one bare leg hanging off the cot, no intention of going anywhere.

"What are you *doing*? You can't stay here! Do you know what will happen if they find out?" I'm not sure myself, but it can't possibly be good, and I'm still convinced that my mother will be told. I have to get him out of the shack unnoticed and I've already wasted too much time.

"Relax. I'll slip out after you go. No one will know I was here." He watches me as I frantically climb back into my uniform, cursing the bad luck of getting the one night they decide to have a drill. Pulling my boots back on I don't even bother to lace them up as I hug Sasha quickly before jogging out the door, across the yard and up the stone steps of the main building where everyone has gathered. I feel like they all know what I have been doing, as I try to tuck stray curls away from my face. The meeting does not last long, and part of me hopes Sasha will still be there when I return. But the room is empty, the only trace remaining a faint scent of leather and cigarettes. I throw myself onto the cot and cry myself to sleep out of sheer frustration.

A week later a soldier appears in the doorway of my make-shift office, her job to escort me to the main building where my presence has been requested. I follow her green clad form, jealous that unlike me, she has managed to make the ungainly uniform look good. On the ground floor I am introduced to the officer who sent her to fetch me, a stocky man with a square jaw and gray eyes that size me up without attempt at disguise. "You'll sit at this desk," he points, before returning to his own room, an open window in the wall affording us a view of each other. I take my seat but only briefly, his deep voice asking for a cup of coffee I didn't realize was included in a job no one has bothered to explain.

My culinary skills leave much to be desired, my mother having always insisted that my time be reserved for studying or practicing the piano. This means that unlike other girls my age, Ronit who bakes wondrous cakes, or Limor who prepares her father's dinner on nights her mother runs late, I can barely crack an egg. But coffee I can make, and within a few moments I have a cup of hot liquid I carry in to my higher up, his boyish head bent over a pile of documents on his desk. He grunts his thanks as I return to my side of the room, where I watch him through the partition. I have been raised in a home where I have been taught to stand up to authority, (not my mother's), to demand respect and expect chivalrous behavior. The officer quickly falls short of this last. After sipping the coffee he rises with cup and saucer in hand, and crosses his room into mine where he strides to the open window through which he pours out the drink. I stare in disbelief.

"Next time, don't put so much milk in my coffee," he states casually as he turns back from the window.

"Next time, you can make it yourself," I retort, my eyes level with his. I hold my breath, waiting for him to react, yell, punish. Instead, it seems I have stunned him into silence.

That afternoon I follow yet another soldier as she escorts me to the top floor of the old building. This time my presence has been requested by the lieutenant colonel. It appears I have been promoted.

*　　*　　*

The view from my new office feels like a gift. Wide glass doors look out over the port of Haifa, the mountain falling away below me filled with old stone buildings and dark pine trees. The sea stretches in the distance, freight ships, tankers and an occasional liner looming against the blue sky. I am shown to my desk, where other than answering the occasional phone call I am left to my own devices. The only other duty expected of me is to wipe down floors when I arrive in the morning, and to sit at my desk until the colonel leaves at night. Early the next day I climb the stairs to my perch and there, windows thrown open and the entire office to myself, I soak the cleaning rag, set my feet on both its ends, and slide across the tile floor. I stop this unorthodox cleaning method only long enough to take in part of the sixth fleet which has materialized in the port below during the night. The USS Eisenhower stretches majestically, its crew like ants scurrying across its impressive expanse as the day begins to warm. American sailors will soon fill Haifa's port, drinking in its bars, visiting with the prostitutes in the seedy streets below. And one afternoon Sara's daughter Limor, will meet a sailor from the Eisenhower and get herself invited on a tour, asking me to come along. I am not sure whether I am chosen out of friendship or because she needs a translator as she lovingly gazes at the sailor's six-foot frame. Her reason does not matter to me. From the boat ride to the ship, to the tour across its expansive flight deck, across every knee knocker between our peek at the sailors' bunks to the mess hall where we are invited to eat, I enjoy every moment of the afternoon, my eyes filled with the beauty of the men's uniforms, while my ears soak up the English I have sorely missed.

Despite my recently acquired status of soldier, my mother still believes she has the final and ultimate say in anything that concerns my well-being. She has begun to question the need for the late hours I am expected to keep at the base, demanding that I ask to be escorted to the bus station when it is time to go home. I try to explain that I can't possibly expect the lieutenant colonel to walk a mere private at the end of each evening.

"If you don't ask him I will." And I panic at the image of my mother showing up at the base and demanding to speak to the man whose door I guard late into the night. I still don't know what it is he does in there, suspecting that my presence is mere decoration from the sounds of laughter coming from behind closed doors. Tonight he has asked me to make Turkish coffee for himself and a group of officers with whom he'd been in his office since late afternoon, assuming that I knew how to brew this traditional drink. I am familiar with its cardamom scent, its thick brown liquid poured into quaint small cups for special customers in the shops of the Druze villages. When my parents visit Ronit's family, her father cooks this aromatic coffee in a *finjan*, a small coffee pot with a long handle held over the flame where he allows it to boil, rising and falling until he pours its foamy thickness and offers it to my father only. The ritual always seems magical to me, a secret between men in which I am not invited to partake. And now I was expected to prepare it for a roomful of men who would probably know the difference if I did not get it right. I nervously eye the counter where the empty *finjan* awaits, recalling the movements of Ronit's father as he filled it with water, then added the finely ground coffee, followed by heaping spoonfuls of sugar. I place the pot on the flame before wandering off to take in the view, the now darkened port twinkling below, its seediness disguised by the moon's glow washing everything beneath it clean. I try to make out the Eisenhower's sleeping form but before my eyes have a chance to focus a hiss and sizzle in the room behind me cause me to spin around just in time to watch the overflowing *finjan* give up its dark secrets. Brown sugary liquid spills over the pot and to the tile floor, a miniature volcano erupting and filling the room with the scent of burnt coffee.

"Never turn your back on Turkish coffee." The lieutenant is standing in his doorway, eyeing the floor and my bewildered face, his right hand on his hip, his left sleeve empty where his arm should have been. I don't know what to say and before I have a chance to apologize he turns on his heel, about to disappear into his room.

"If you need me to stay late tonight, I'd like someone to walk me to the bus station." I can't believe I said it but my mother's threat holds greater power than the stripes and decorations on the colonel's uniform. He pauses in the doorway, his back still turned.

"You can go. Your security cleared; Report to your new base tomorrow." And just like that my time on this mountain is up and I am about to begin the next phase of my military career. I watch the colonel close the door without a further glance in my direction. I stay just long enough for a quick mop of the sticky floor and a last look at the glittering view before I head out to the bus station, alone.

Good

I'm told to be good so many times I start to wonder what being bad must be like. Maybe it's like beautiful Aunt Iris who there in my mother's living room, sits on my uncle's lap, one thin tan arm wrapped casually around his neck, manicured red nails playing with the hair at his nape. She smugly ignores the daggers in my mother's eyes as well as her muttered "We have chairs in this house," and in that instant wins my undying respect. "Be proper," mother says. "Be ladylike," she instructs. "Stop staring!" My grandmother warns, in a women's dressing room at the beach, where I don't know where to look to avoid breasts. "A train could go through there!" My mother chastises, and I know that I must be sitting splay legged and unladylike. My posture is reason for concern as well, as if there, in the curve of my spine lays the possibility of bad deeds, the straighter the back the less chance of my misbehaving. But I'm starting to recognize a hidden power I think I must have. I see it in the insolent dark eyes of the man selling flowers by the bus stop when I return from dance class one night. And some time ago, the Bedouin man at the campground wash-basin smiled toothily and asked my mother "How much for the girl?" Causing her to wrap me up and whisk me away in the big red towel she bought at Sears a few years back in California. And of course I have realized that the men I have briefly dated find me attractive for more than my uniqueness as a foreigner of sorts. I haven't used my powers yet, not until the night I lie to my mother. I promise Sasha to meet him at the bus stop across the road from my new base. "Come with me, just for tonight," he persuades; those blue eyes

I misread promising to love me forever, or to leave me if I deny him. And I believe those eyes and his promises as I concoct my elaborate tale.

"I'll be staying at a friend's house tonight," I tell my mother. "I'll call you when I get there," which I do, from a public phone in another city. And just like that, I am free.

Until Sara's daughter, Limor tells my mother that she saw me earlier that afternoon, boarding a bus going in the opposite direction. But by then it's too late. My mother's hothouse flower has been checked into a little bungalow by the sea on the outskirts of the ancient crusade city of Acre. And under Napoleon's not so watchful gaze, his iron silhouette atop the hill he tried to conquer, I learn to please someone other than my mother. The good girl in me becomes a lover, my cries of pain unheeded as they mingle with the crashing of the sea outside the window. And at that moment I know that nothing will ever be the same again. I enter a world in which I can finally be that hidden me. She's the one who wears red lipstick and paints her long nails the crimson of the hibiscus flowers. She's the one who sings out loud without her cheeks burning red, and dances to the wild drum beat always pounding in her ears. Not the timid girl summoned by mother to play the piano for guests. That other me, the one who breaks all my mother's rules, runs across the train tracks any chance she gets, into neighborhoods where old Russian babushkas still drink their tea with sugar cubes between their gold capped teeth. I ache with want and these neighborhoods call to me, warm people who insist I am part of their family now that I have made their son so happy. I sit among them, at tables covered with embroidered linen under delicate etched glasses brimming with Vodka, bowls of herring, plates of smoked fish, all offered to the skinny Israeli. Raucous and raunchy are their jokes; loud and heartfelt is their laughter, their language and warmth washing over me like a benediction.

Top Secret

Israel, Winter 1984

J ust when I thought that the army green uniform, that great equalizer would make me belong, I am again separated from the herd, this time in ways I had not anticipated. Once past the heavily armed guards at the entrance to my new base, the parking lot teeming with civilian and military personnel alike, our small group of soldiers is gathered for an informal roll call conducted by Anat, the petite blonde officer responsible for us for the next two years.

Despite the uniform, the early hour and the official clipboard she holds, there is something casual in the officer's stance, her delicate blue eye shadow an indication that she is more woman than soldier. Her uniform shirt is neatly tucked into her narrow pants, a wide belt cinching a slim waist, and on her feet are simple black pumps, small heels adding a feminine touch to the otherwise unflattering ensemble. I am made all too aware of my own feet, strapped into leather sandals and white socks, a combination that would earn me the title of dork had my American friend Maggie been present to disapprove.

Her brief lecture over, the officer sends us to our individual assignments, girls breaking off in pairs and threesomes for secretarial work in various offices in the enormous expanse that is my new base. I gaze after them for a moment before heading the opposite way; their lilting voices fading as I start my daily trek down a sandy road on which no movement other than an occasional speeding military jeep can be seen for long stretches in either direction. My knowledge of English has earned me entrance into a remote and narrow building that resembles temporary classrooms that schools erect when space is scarce. I have been given a special code which has to be punched in before the heavy door pops open with a metallic click. Once inside, the thinly carpeted hallway leads me past several doors behind which is conducted business that I am forbidden to speak of to anyone.

"Not to your friends, not your parents, not even to any of the other soldiers in your unit. Do you have a boyfriend?"

"Yes."

"Not to him, either." These instructions are given in a low, solemn voice by the short civilian seated behind a desk in the corner office. I take him seriously even before my eyes are drawn to the rope noose hanging from the ceiling in the right hand corner behind him. He knows I've seen it and it won't be mentioned until the day I leave, when he will debrief me and warn, pointing to the noose, that I shall speak to no one of what I've seen and heard within these walls. On that last day he will make me sign a document promising not to set foot in any Arab countries for the next five years. He will also hand me a small note with a number which he says I should call if I am ever in need of help. "All you have to do is call it and he will come." By then I will have lost my initial enthusiasm for the cloak and dagger atmosphere of my job, and all I will think as I reach for the piece of paper is that the man must have watched one too many spy movies. I don't even ask who this "he" may be, and what kind of trouble I am expected to get into once I leave.

For now, there are a handful of men whose needs I will be fulfilling for months to come, men whose habits and quirks I will come to know as well as my own. Little is explained to me about the documents crossing my desk, but after a few weeks of translating, typing, appointment making and listening to snippets of conversation that drift into my room, the picture of which I have been made a part comes into focus. I realize that despite their jokes and flirtatiousness, the men who occupy this container in which we spend most of our days are dealing in state of the art armaments for the Israeli defense force. Those bits and pieces of conversation that had sounded elusive and colorful just a few weeks ago now represent a dangerous menu of weaponry that these men are creating, testing and selling to various entities overseas. Once I understand what they actually are, "Sharks" and "Pythons" do more than slither and swim past my desk. They now explode and counter attacks for which these missiles that they are were built. When I learn that the word "Matador" on an official form is really a wall breaching device, it no longer conjures up images of Spain and angry bulls. My new vocabulary is filled with precision guided weapons, jamming systems, iron domes and combat suits, and I am grateful to hear the metallic click of the door behind me at the end of each day.

*   *   *

When the novelty of my new surroundings and job wears off, I start wondering whether the legend that all bases have holes in their fences holds true for this fortress, as well. I have heard rumors of a breach along a fence line that lets out onto an alley in a familiar neighborhood. If I can find the spot I will know where to go from there. On a day when work has slowed to a crawl and half of the men are out of the country, armed with the etiquette packets I had prepared for whichever culture with which they were wheeling and dealing, I decide to venture out and explore. I reason that no one will miss me at lunch, since I seldom join the other girls and they are not allowed into my building without prior arrangement. My plan is to put the legend to the test and find the hole, if there is one; then walk to Sasha's apartment to surprise him, making sure to return on time for roll call at the end of the day. The base is flanked by the main road to one side and by the Mediterranean on the other, and somewhere in the direction of the beach is Sasha's neighborhood, my determination to see him growing as I gather my purse and lock the door behind me.

I make my way down paths that become increasingly sandier, an indication that I am heading in the right direction. The landscape is dotted with buildings from which I hear an occasional ringing of metallic instruments, yet otherwise, little if any sounds are heard in the late morning air. Following where the path leads I notice the sudden appearance of a barbed wire fence running the length of the road and into the distance. I let out a small shriek when the large head of a German shepherd lunges towards me, its deep warning bark sending me scurrying the rest of the way, as other guard dogs emerge from dog houses I can see from the corner of my eye as I race along. I slow down to catch my breath just long enough to wonder at the strange metallic contraptions whose tops I can see peeking over the stone wall to my left. They look like an odd breed of giraffes, their heads reminiscent of gun barrels as they stare at me from behind their enclosure.

I have been away from my desk for about twenty minutes now, enough time to put the strangeness of this military world out of my mind and allow myself to fantasize about the afternoon ahead. I can imagine Sasha's surprised expression when he opens the door to find me standing there; the way he will pull me in close enough to feel his heart beat through his thin frame; the narrow bed in which we will share a languid afternoon, wintry light and sea air drifting through his eighth floor window. I shake myself out of my reverie to pay attention to my surroundings, beginning to worry that perhaps all I'll get to do is fantasize if the hole doesn't actually exist. I start searching in earnest now, until a gravelly sound of tires takes me by surprise. A military jeep is fast approaching and my heart lurches into my throat as I realize what may happen when I'm found so far from my desk. As the vehicle slows and the sand it has kicked up settles, I see four grinning faces leering out at me, the two soldiers in the back twisted around in their seats to see what they've stumbled across.

"Ahalan. Need a ride?" The driver's left arm is casually draped over the steering wheel, his right hand gripped around the stick shift of the idling jeep, a knowing look in his smiling eyes.

"Yes – that'd be great. Thanks." My mind is on autopilot, and my body follows as the driver gestures for me to climb into the back where I join the other two passengers and an open crate of fish whose dead eyes look up at me accusingly. The jeep lurches forward without warning before my bottom has touched the narrow bench, and I grip the side to avoid tumbling out. I realize that I have no idea where the driver is headed, nor did he ask where I was going. Yet my shyness coupled with the whistling of the wind through the open jeep prevents me from speaking up and I sit back against the metal bars, along for the bumpy ride regardless of its destination. It isn't long however, before I realize that we are aiming for the main gate, and panic grips me once more since I have no permission to leave in case anyone asks. I can already make out the low roof under which we all take turns standing guard in the mornings, checking identification cards, matching the faces of civilians and military personnel alike to photos hanging from lanyards around their necks before admitting them onto the base. We are nearly level with the guard at the front gate, his machine gun cradled casually along the inner length of his right arm, and I feel the sudden urge to jump out and head back before questions have to be answered. But before

I give way to my impulse the guard lifts his left hand in a casual greeting, and waves us forward without a second glance in my direction; A miracle.

"We're heading for Motzkin, will that work for you?" The driver yells back his question, and I nod agreement, not trusting that the wind will carry my answer to its intended target. Motzkin is the suburb between Sasha's and my own, where my mother works as a nurse at the elementary school I will have to circumnavigate to avoid being seen. She comes home with tales of skinned knees and lice-ridden Georgian girls whose fathers forbid them to cut their hip length hair. She also deals with a Russian custodian who has taken to drinking the rubbing alcohol in her supply cabinet. Glancing back I no longer see the base we have just left, fragrant Eucalyptus trees hiding its walls with their lanky forms. I watch grey apartment buildings as we fly by, curious about the lives being conducted in each one right now, wondering who else is where they're not supposed to be. Up ahead I can already recognize the small shops that line the road where my ride comes to an end, the vendors' displays of bright vegetables and colorful flowers lending the otherwise drab surroundings a festive air.

"You have a good afternoon now." The driver waits just long enough for me to climb down and step away from the jeep's side before he swoops back out into traffic, carrying his cargo of soldiers and fish on some less than official military business I am hardly in a position to question. My thank you is swallowed in the rush of cars and I make my way across the road, hoping not to be recognized by any housewives out shopping for the evening's dinner. Ours is a small country and news travels fast, especially news of daughters behaving badly. Despite our frequent departures from this country and my generally poor sense of direction, the map of the surrounding neighborhoods is embedded in my mind's eye, every step of the way between the heavy door of our house and the front door of Sasha's apartment laid out in intricate detail. Like an inmate memorizing an escape plan, I know every twist and turn between our two doors, the feel of every railing my hands have gripped, the number of steps between the railroad tracks and the forested park where we meet on warm summer nights, taking refuge in the dark. Within minutes I have left the bustling stores behind in exchange for rows of apartment buildings, their fronts studded with balconies from which hang rugs and mattresses to air in the sun. Just ahead is a small mall, quiet and empty until the elementary school directly behind it will let out and children will fill its tiled expanse buying ice cream and sweets before heading home. I glance up at the building to my left, my eyes traveling instinctively to the fourth floor where Sasha's best friend, Moshe lives with his aging parents. I half expect his tall frame to emerge from his bedroom window, like it does every Friday night when we gather in the parking lot below and the boys whistle for him to come down. No one makes a move without the other, the small group of friends all recent Russian immigrants, their newness and their heavy accents uniting them against any possible threat from natives and other newcomers alike. I am the exception they have allowed in; an Israeli and the only girl among them.

I continue down sidewalks flanked by low stone walls and familiar plants, the light blue *plumbago* a favorite among children for its sticky flowers, good for throwing at each other or dangling from earlobes as makeshift earrings. I trail my hand through its fragrant softness, too lost in contemplation to notice the car that has slowed to a crawl behind me. Its driver does not appear to be parking, nor are they in any hurry to rejoin traffic. Instead the car follows me like a faithful dog, and I know who is behind the wheel before I even bother to turn and verify. We could continue like this indefinitely, and eventually I would cross the railroad tracks and be out of reach unless she follows me on foot. But I already feel slightly ridiculous and self-conscious, and our odd procession is bound to attract unwanted attention. I turn, my movements as slow as molasses prolonging my fate. Anat watches me from behind the windshield, her expression stoic as she leans out her window and motions me to approach. I am strangely calm considering the consequences she would be in her rights to enforce, and the entire encounter has a dream-like quality, as though it is not actually happening to me but to a character I am watching from a safe distance.

"You know you don't have my permission to be here," she says. I suppose stating the obvious is necessary under such circumstances.

"I know. I needed to see my boyfriend." No point making up excuses now.

"We'll talk about this when you get back." I'm sure we will, followed by a weekend detention or a court martial and jail time, depending on her mood. Sara's daughter, Limor, who has a year's experience at the base, had told me of such punishments for smaller transgressions. Finally, I think to myself, I will be treated like everyone else, what I always wanted. Yet nothing of the sort happens. Instead, it will take weeks of jumping at every ring of the office phone, certain I was being summoned to accept my consequences, until I realize that no punishment was coming. I will never find out why.

"I'll see you tomorrow." Anat does not sound angry, just tired, as she rolls her window back up, signals, and pulls out into the lane, leaving me standing in surprise at not being told to get in to her car so she can return me to the base. Five months from now I'll wish she had.

Sin

Israel, Spring 1985

There in the narrow storage shed, dimly lit by one bare
bulb swaying above us, Lee and I are perched on over-
turned crates, waiting for the results of a cheap preg-
nancy test. She looks as nervous as I feel, her left hand clasping a
watch while she chews absentmindedly on the nails of her right
fingers. I am already preparing for the worse, thinking of ways
to escape if the result is positive. Yet where does one hide in a
neighborhood full of eyes watching, tongues reporting, mother
waiting for me to disgrace as I surely will, all the tell-tale signs already show where I am headed. "Why are you holding hands like
babies?" She mocks if I dare allow a boyfriend to show affection.
"Why do you chase pants?" her response for my inexplicable
need for male company; Now this. The final proof that I am my
father's daughter, this horrible interest in sex passed down to me
despite her puritan attempts to keep me clean.

The beeping from Lee's watch sends me out of my reverie
and we both stare at the indicator, unable to make out its color
in the darkness of the shed. "I think it's negative, I'm not sure…"
and I put all my faith in my worldly friend and her reading of
my future. I swear her to secrecy even though she would never
betray me, years of loyal friendship proof of this. Lee who has
been a willing participant in every scheme I have suggested, her
story telling abilities at my disposal for any gaps in time in which
my mother could not place me. And as the years go by and my
mother's reins tighten, my need for these uncensored moments

grows. I leave the shed with a lighter heart, although a voice is telling me that I've only postponed what is bound to come. Weeks later a neighbor eyes me with suspicion as I pass under her balcony and within minutes I am confronted by my mother, shamed by the neighbor's suggestion that she take me to a doctor. My mother's questioning is brief, conducted in an unusually calm demeanor, the result a visit to an obscure doctor in the next suburb, where no one knows whose daughter and granddaughter I am. My father takes me, my mother too worried she might be recognized, and we make our way in silence, up the elevator of an aging apartment building where old Russian women eye us knowingly as we pass them on the landing. We are shown in by a slender, balding man in his undershirt, who waves us to a scantily furnished living room where others already wait. A middle-aged woman sits with a small child fidgeting on her lap. A young woman stares at the pages of a magazine she clearly isn't reading, not having turned a page since we'd arrived. A man is seated near her but I can't tell if they are together, his face a cross between anger and boredom. I don't want to look at my father who has kept his silence this entire time. Instead I fix my eyes on the peeling wallpaper, allowing my gaze to follow its pattern of flowers I don't recognize and try to name. But before I can decide whether the petals look like poppies or petunias, a gruff looking woman signals me to follow her into a small room down the hall. I dare a glance at my father who smiles weakly, and turn my back on all the inquisitive eyes watching me make my way across the makeshift waiting room. Once inside, I am asked to lie down on the examination table, where I focus my gaze on the yellowing ceiling and my ears on the sounds of traffic outside the window behind me. The doctor, her hands cold and her accent thick, is businesslike in her questions, quick with her exam, and visibly angered at her findings. She cannot understand how I have kept this secret to myself all this time.

On our way down, the elevator still smells of cheap perfume and stale cigarettes, and the look on my father's face is full of sorrow at the news he will have to reveal to my mother and the inevitable decision she will make.

Appearances

Israel, 1985

The hospital room looks out towards Haifa, and from my position on the bed I can see lights beginning to twinkle, as evening lowers itself on to the mountain. I imagine families gathering for dinner, mothers in fragrant kitchens, fathers reading the paper, the evening news reporting the latest casualties. Ordinary lives taking place outside my window. I've been left alone, waiting for the saline to do its work. My mother is away, attending my brother's violin concert. Not appearing would lead to questions and keeping this disgrace secret is of utmost importance. After all, appearances are everything and we have a name to uphold. The doctor, his face kinder than I expected, had seemed surprised when he first bent over me. "You're not the kind of girl I usually see," he said, and I wondered who had preceded me on that cold examination table and whether he had been kind to her, too. "I usually restrain the girls before I inject them, but if you promise not to move, I'd rather not do that to you." Another kindness and I wonder what I've done to deserve it. A sudden thought occurs to me, more frightening than the needle he is preparing. What if he's being nice because he knows who my grandmother is? The doctor merely doing a favor for a colleague? But my mother would never admit to such failure, her perfect daughter behaving like a common whore.

I am jerked out of my thoughts by the doctor who is again at my side, explaining what he is about to do. Is he deliberately slow? Or is it my imagination tricking me into believing that he's hoping I will change my mind? Downstairs, earlier that morning, a woman in an army uniform had already tried to sway me from my decision. "There are other ways to do this. Does the father of the baby know?" But I was well rehearsed, my mother's instructions in my mouth. "No need to tell him. Why make another person suffer?" I say my lines, earning a compliment I do not deserve. "How very thoughtful of you to protect his feelings." Another lie since I would like nothing more than to run across the train tracks and up to the eighth floor apartment where he lives and be saved. But my mother, standing in the corridor behind the closed door, has warned that if I defy her I will no longer be her daughter, and I am still under her spell.

Now upstairs, I look away from the needle in the doctor's hand, my face to the whitewashed wall his signal to proceed. "You'll feel a small pinch, then a burning sensation," he explains, inserting the solution low into my abdomen. His hand is dry and fatherly as he helps me off the table and out the door, back to the room upstairs where I am to wait for this shame to be gone. Hours later when the pain begins, it is the kind doctor I scream for, and the efficient nurse who earlier answered all the questions my mother would not, assures me that this will be over soon, and did I have any other questions? Between waves of pain I thank her for her kindness, treasuring the frankness with which she had explained what my body already knew to do. If only my mother could have spoken to me this way. Instead, the only answer she had supplied to my naïve "how will it come out?" was a thin lipped "the same way it went in," the rest of the bus ride to the hospital made in silence. The nurse has appeared again, tight faced and silent as she whisks away what I am straining to see. By the time my mother enters the room, she has already been told that my commanding officer has been to visit me, and she is searching for the nurse who disobeyed the clear orders she had left not to let anyone know I am here. But I am glad he had cared enough to find me, an important man like him taking time out of his busy day for a soldier from his unit. It was the first time I had seen him looking awkward, standing in the doorway with his hat between his hands, asking if I was all right. I had lied to him too, my knees pulled up to hide the mound of my stomach, mother's instructions if anyone were to come in, and promised I'd be back at the base soon.

In my mother's absence the morning sun has lit a dozen fires in the windows of the buildings on mount Haifa, where children are being sent off to school, soldiers are waiting for the bus, and daughters don't have to lie to keep their mother's good name clean.

*   *   *

My mother's solution to my immediate and overwhelming depression is the acquisition of a dog. And as much as I love animals, I can't help but feel resentment at the idea that being given a puppy will in any way make up for the loss of a child as well as a lover I am now forbidden to see. Even my interactions with girlfriends are monitored, Lee's visit to my bedside the day after my return from the hospital cut short when my mother overhears her commenting about my paleness.

"She's been sick, nothing serious. She'll be better in a few days," my mother hurries to say while Lee and I exchange knowing looks, amazed that my mother is naïve enough to believe I haven't told my friend everything; Amazed that after years of living in this neighborhood she does not know that I am the topic of dinner conversations in most of the surrounding apartments. For the few moments we get to visit, I almost feel normal again, Lee's hand on mine as she sits beside me on the bed calming and sincere. I would have liked her to stay, my need to talk about the past two days welling in my throat. But I am also in disgrace, and so have lost the right to complain.

On a gray fall morning my mother and I drive out of town towards the industrial stretch of factories and refineries where the local animal shelter is kept. Shaky tin roofs and makeshift walls enclose a row of cages in which raggedy creatures are waiting for adoption, some despondent, having given up all hope, while others throw themselves at the chain link fence as we walk past. My eyes fall on a cage in which a handful of dark pups are scampering over each other, and I ask the attendant to unlock the enclosure so I can make my selection. A black shaggy runt attracts my attention, and within minutes the transaction is complete and the small warm body is on my lap as my mother points the car towards home.

By the time evening falls, the happy puppy I had selected is refusing water and food, its body nearly lifeless. A rushed visit to the vet confirms distemper, a disease from which the vet explains few if any dogs survive. This turn of events only worsens my depression, convincing me that I am not meant to handle life in any form. However, my mother sees it as a challenge she must overcome to prove her nursing skills. For days she injects the pup with the nutrients it needs, efficient and practical in her handling of all things weak. And to everyone's surprise but her own, the dog recovers, now capable of carrying out its intended task of cheering me up. Instead, while I will grow attached to the animal and insist on traveling with it to America, my mother will forever remind anyone willing to listen how she saved the dog when it was beyond saving. Just like the daughter who strayed and was almost lost until her mother came to the rescue; saving her from everything she loved.

My Father's Decision

Israel, 1986

It couldn't have been an easy one to make. I know, because a few years later I made it, too. And once again, as with any major decision in our past, my mother set this one on its irreversible course. That silent lament my father carried with him through the house was louder than he imagined it to be, because I heard it. In the silences he chose to meet my mother's demands, in the muteness I faced when asking him to speak to her on my behalf. It drifted up the staircase from the study where he kept himself to himself, and shared less and less with us. After my unspeakable act, when mother decided I needed to be saved, ("You've done things that should not be done,") America was once again the destination. Only this time my father was being left behind, her need for him negligible compared to the dangers she thought I faced. She could only imagine what would happen if we were to remain in this country that had corrupted the daughter for whom she held such high hopes. My release from the military could not come soon enough, a forced vacation they insisted I take the only delay in my mother's rush to board a plane. My father would join us in due time once he completed his job at the university in Haifa, my mother was certain of this, while she accompanied me into my future away from him. Away from the boy who started all this trouble, the one I could still smell on my skin. Sasha, waiting on that bench we had declared our own, in the quiet park where pools of blue lamplight held us in their tranquil glow. I was being uprooted from all that was familiar and dear, prevented from even telling him I was leaving the country.

Left alone, my father wandered the silent house, its walls still echoing my mother's disappointment in me, and his own disappointment for failing to speak up. Yet with this silence came freedom. Free rein to wear what he wanted, say whatever pleased him, feel the way his heart dictated without censor. On his first summer visit to California before Israel calls him back, a man exits the plane and I barely recognize my father behind the salt and pepper beard that had not been there before. I hug his tired frame, laugh at the new roughness of his beard against my face, and watch in dismay as my mother stops him with an outstretched arm before he has a chance to greet her too.

"I am not kissing you until you shave that off" she declares, and I am angered and offended for him, angry with my mother for treating him unkindly, saddened when I see his clean-shaven yet defeated face later that afternoon.

In a few years, when his assignment as department chair ends and the time comes to join us, to walk back in to the cage that had been his life, my father will have to make a choice. He will have to leave a country he had grown to love to replace it with one on the other side of the world, and he will have had enough of feeling like a newly arrived immigrant. A woman who accepts him the way he is will replace the one he could never seem to satisfy. And for a man who had escaped Hungary at age fourteen, whose life had felt like a refugee's ever since, one place to call home was the most charming life imaginable. Not the shuttling between countries, between houses, the gypsy life that seemed to feed my mother's restless nature.

His decision seems inevitable when I look back. His need to stay in the land that couldn't seem to hold my mother, the country that had first impressed him with its cloudless blue skies and its flowering Jacaranda trees. He will return. To another family, to another man's wife, to a new garden he would now call his own. And my mother's perfect family will fall apart. She will no longer be able to pretend that we are immune once we become those people discussed by others in low tones and a shaking of heads. "Did you hear about what happened? And their daughter? Who would have thought, such a nice family..." furtive exchanges of information as hands reached for milk at the grocery store. Quiet updates as housewives bent over the fruit stand to check the sweetness of the grapes. Despite all my mother's efforts to keep appearances, we will become the stuff of cheap novels, straying husbands and wayward daughters filling their pages. And America would save us.

One parent in America, one parent in Israel. A brother no longer speaking to his father, having declared his allegiance elsewhere. A father who years later during a brief visit to America, would stand on the sidewalk of a busy street, just to catch a glimpse of his son through an office window on the opposite side. And a daughter, torn between two lands, choosing sides, declaring loyalties. A family divided, scattering to the winds, like the wild poppies whose pods needed only the slightest touch before they split their sides and burst open, seeds scattering every which way.

Senses

Like long time lovers, my land and I trace each other's contours in our sleep, no longer surprised by what our touch may find. In the cities I walk through in my mind, I feel the polished roughness of Jerusalem stone, block upon carved block creating the city of my birth. On the beaches of my childhood, I hear the gentle lapping of waves as they wash the morning to shore. In my dreams, I breathe in the perfume of pulsing city streets, bus fumes mingling with the steamy vapors rising from vats of boiling corn. A few steps more and I will see the glimmering lights of Haifa's port, reaching out to welcome me as they have done before. And underfoot my toes sink in to sun warmed sand, hurrying me towards cooling waves of saltiness where I am drawn to dance until my limbs are tangled in the sea's embrace. But like any dream, this one too must come to its ephemeral end, the seductive past disappearing like phantoms on the breeze through my bedroom window. And like all great loves, it forever leaves me wanting more.

Immigrants

We're not your garden-variety used-to-live-some-
where-else immigrants. And any time Americans
want to know where I'm from, I feel like making
something up, just to make my answer easier to understand.
"How long have you been here?" They ask. Because they can
tell, from the way my hair curls, the precise way I pronounce my
words like I've taken a bite of a favorite dessert and I'm trying to
make it last. They can tell I don't really belong. If I say I'm from
here, on days I don't want to be from anywhere else, people look
disappointed, their one chance to touch something exotic taken
away. But the true answer isn't easy to follow. Unlike other immigrants who left all that was dear and familiar behind and replanted themselves in a new land, our family can't seem to make
up its mind. My mother wants America for my father's sake, so
she says. He has been invited to study and work, and America
will make him successful. Then nostalgia, that elixir all immigrants keep stashed away to furtively sip when what used to be
home calls their name, hits my mother hard and makes us pack
and return; To another apartment, another war, another stab at
being Israeli. I speak both languages and my face is familiar in
both lands; the transformation from one self to another becoming routine, an actor donning the right mask and rehearsing the
correct script before the curtain rises.

But there are days, more and more of them, when I want you
to look at me and see *America*, hear *America*. So I wear the jeans,
apply the make-up, shave the Mediterranean from my skin. I

rein in the tongue straining at the bit. But how do I tame the wild hair, teach it to lie down and fit in with all the well-behaved blond heads around? How do I silence the sharp tongue that has been conditioned to fight back at the least offense? I have to practice wearing the face that gives away nothing. I learn to slow the blood ready to boil over. But try as I may, I cannot paint this Anglo world on my Israeli face, put American pleasantries on a desert tongue. Many years will have to pass before I learn the steps to this unfamiliar dance.

*   *   *

California, 1987

My mother has decided to take in boarders despite the money my father sends from Israel on a monthly basis. Perhaps she wants to feel as if she is doing her fair share. Perhaps she already has her eye on the larger house down the street where we will move before my father returns. Whatever her reasoning, she places an advertisement in the local paper, and soon my brother and I are sharing the master bedroom with our mother, while strangers move into the two rooms in which we used to sleep.

The woman who is now occupying what used to be my room is large in every sense of the word. She walks around the house in a billowy nightgown, her thick ankles loosely stuffed into slippers in which she shuffles down the corridor. Her notion of renting a room includes standing beside our dining room table as we have our breakfast, loudly expressing political opinions as we try to watch the morning news. My mother is uncharacteristically restrained in her reactions, the woman's monthly check incentive for silence. Within a few days my brother's room is occupied as well by a tall thin man who insists on having the central heating on at night despite the armful of blankets my mother leaves on his bed.

"I don't like heavy blankets on my body when I sleep," he offers in explanation to my mother's questioning. And once more she gives in, reserving her complaints about how strange Americans are for me as we lie sweltering in our beds, in a room from which I feel there is no escape other than the blessed few hours a day during which I attend the local university. I dread returning to a house in which I now feel like a guest, where I have no room of my own to which I can close the door on the dramas of my mother's life. The home and mother to which I have been conditioned to be loyal are now an oppressive prison. Unlike the familiar Israeli landscape in which I can clearly picture at least half a dozen safe havens as I lie in bed in my mother's room dreaming of escape, I can't imagine even one place where I can hide or one person to whom I can turn on this side of the world.

*   *   *

Sitting in American classrooms is not new to me. After all, I have been doing so off and on since age five, when all that was expected of us in Mrs. Boda's kindergarten was that we play well with others on the wooden structure and nap quietly on mats in the afternoons. By the time I arrive on the campus of the University of Davis in California, my English is correct if halting, my tongue unaccustomed to living so many hours of the day in a language until now reserved for book reports, translation of documents, and reading of eighteenth century novels. For the first few semesters I sit through courses in comparative literature and classics, straining to keep up with my second language which still flies by too quickly. I worry that a professor will say something I will not be able to understand, worse yet, that I will be asked a question and not be able to respond while everyone sits waiting. I am self-conscious at age twenty-one in a way I had not been when I was in Mrs. Sherry's sixth grade, where my love for words was encouraged when the students were asked to write our own small book of poetry. For days I walked around our rented apartment, rhyming and tinkering with words that I proudly pieced together, forming my creations out of imagination and English. In ninth grade and back in California again, I was lucky enough to be placed in Mrs. Tichinin's English class where I was introduced to Shakespeare, memorizing entire passages I played over and over in my head as I biked home from school, as I lay in my bed drifting off to sleep, Juliet's voice bidding Romeo "…a thousand times good night…." Other students had warned me that Mrs. Tichinin was the strictest teacher on campus, intimidated by her weathered face that matched the leather pants she wore, her long white hair flowing wildly behind her. But I was a lover of language, and Mrs. Tichinin recognized the hunger with which I swallowed the words she set before me.

Soon living in English stops being strange, my need for it spilling into friendships I make, into songs I sing along with the university choir I join. I sit more comfortably in my classrooms, no longer on the edge of my chair ready to catch those quick words that fall from professors' mouths, ready to escape out the door if I miss. Yet I still need to return home at the end of each day and become me in Hebrew, my sounds different, my voice no longer the confident young woman's in the English of the outside world. Once home, I return to my mother, to my mother tongue, in which the rules are still upheld despite the freedom I enjoy while away. More and more English words begin studding my Hebrew as my two halves battle to create a sound that will include both my Israeli and American selves. And neither one is ready yet to sacrifice itself for the sake of the other.

Americans

California, 1989

I can tell my mother is nervous because she has the airport look on her face, the "don't speak unless you are spoken to let me do the talking," look. The only difficulty with this plan is that for a brief period of time, she and I will be separated, and the man seated across the desk at the federal building will actually insist that I speak.

The day has come for our citizenship test, to determine if we are worthy of becoming Americans. So far the immigration building and its officials have done their best to make us feel like outsiders, drab walls and unsmiling clerks unwelcoming to the handful of immigrants seated on hard plastic chairs in the waiting room. When our names are called my mother grimaces at the mispronunciation of mine, Caren sounding like Karen, her own fault for spelling it that way. For a brief moment I wait for her voice to correct, set the clerk straight by pointing out their error. But it does not come. She must want what is promised behind that door even more than her need to prove other people's ignorance.

The man behind the desk is polite but all business. Between questions about the number of stripes on the American flag and what the fourth of July means, I try to read his face but fail. My time in these United States and my exposure to its men has been too brief to help me decipher masked Anglo expressions. Mediterranean men hide nothing, their emotions writ large for all to see. Teachers yell their dissatisfaction, bus drivers growl their stops, strangers flirt shamelessly, their dark eyes following a young woman's moves, desire licking at her heels like hungry flames. The blue-eyed official seems satisfied with my answers, making a few notes before surprising me by reaching across the desk to shake my hand, congratulating me for successfully responding.

Within days my mother and I are standing in a judge's chambers, our right hands over our hearts, about to pledge our allegiance to this country that has opened its doors and welcomed us in. In a few years' time I will be almost indistinguishable from other citizens. My English will no longer be halting, my responses more natural, not script like as I read prepared passages I write out before making a phone call, however simple. I will learn to enjoy the quiet of a suburban afternoon, no neighbors peering into our windows, showing up uninvited for coffee. I will remember to buy my swimsuit when the smell of snow still lingers in the air, quickly learning that the good ones are gone once summer sales arrive. One day I will sit on a grassy hill surrounded by other Americans, waiting for darkness to fall and fireworks to explode across the night sky. And I will feel the pride swelling inside me, understanding the words a roomful of newcomers are now repeating in various accents, some with tears in their eyes. I know that it is good to finally be Americans, our presence in this country no longer legally challenged, although my mother's thick accent will always earn her impatient looks from those claiming they cannot understand her. Yet I'm not certain I am prepared for the declaration we are all making, absolutely and entirely renouncing all allegiance and fidelity to the place from which we came. "I take this obligation freely without any mental reservation...so help me God." But I *do* have reservations, and *which* god? The one before whom old Jewish men in long black coats sway and rock, their prayers floating out the windows of the synagogue down our boulevard, children swinging from the branches of the gnarled fig tree outside? Or the one all our American neighbors celebrate as they gather round twinkling, tinseled trees framed in windows of houses to which we have yet to be invited.

I'm not finished being me in the country I left, haven't had enough time watching older Israeli girls to see if I want to be like them. And now I was expected to be American, simply because our green cards had expired and mother thought the timing right.

Not yet. Not when I still ache for the warmth of a Mediterranean beach under my bare feet, for the rosy sky of an Israeli sunrise, doves cooing on my window's ledge, for my best friend's laugh when I tell a joke in the language in which I still dream. Not when my father's absence is welling up and filling my own eyes here in this room during a ceremony of which he is not a part nor will ever be.

I don't know how to be American. Years still need to pass before I'll adopt the easy banter, slightly dropping the literary English with which so many non-native speakers give themselves away. Years before being referred to as *you guys* doesn't make me cringe and correct the waiter showing me to my seat. I refuse to use the word *cool*, and the beautiful cowboy boots my American husband will buy me one day don't grace my closet yet. I still believe the clerk at the grocery store really wants to know when she asks how I'm doing, and when the friend I just met says she'll talk to me later, I wait for the phone to ring all afternoon before I realize I must have misunderstood.

I was a work in progress in Israel, watching others for clues to tell me who to be. And now I have a wardrobe filled with too many selves, and I don't know which one to wear.

Being Social

California, 1990

My life at this point consists of schoolwork, making up for lost time, since other students my age had already begun their university studies, while I was sporting a green army uniform and an Uzi. I still have every intention of returning to my mother's house at the end of each day, her rules so engrained that I don't allow myself to imagine life on my own, the way other young Americans live. My mother has decided that I need to be social, meet other Jewish people my age. "Why don't you try going to Hillel House? I'm sure you'll meet some nice people there." She persists until I give in, allowing her to drive me the few blocks from our house, dropping me off with an encouraging smile I try to match but fail. She should have let me stay in Israel where my social life would have been guaranteed.

Inside the dilapidated house the small room is crowded, and my chest tightens as I realize I am overdressed. Girls in tight jeans and t-shirts drape themselves over battered sofa arms, chatting easily with young men sipping beer out of large plastic red cups. A few Israeli flags hang from the curtain rods, while Chava Alberstein sings of lost love somewhere in the background. I stand self-consciously in the skirt and blouse I chose for the occasion, recalling the hours of preparation my Israeli girl friends invested before heading out for a social gathering. Here I look like an immigrant. I am about to turn towards the door when my attention is caught by a young man whose broad shoulders tower over the crowd. He looks nothing like the other men in the room, their slim frames reminding me too much of the men in my family. He turns as if on cue, his eyes on mine, and makes his way across the room, a shy smile playing at the corners of his mouth. My eyes are on his hands, pleased to see their large size, blunt nails adorning thick fingers. In seconds my right hand is enveloped in his warm, dry grip as he introduces himself in a deep pleasing voice. "I'm Daniel. Do you want to get out of here?" I nod, following him out into the night without question. His face registers only slight surprise as I get into his car, trusting this stranger because of his wholesome American looks and strong hands.

But this is as far as my stab at independence goes. When he asks what I'd like to do, I suggest driving to my mother's house, where I risk her disapproval at what she is sure to see as brazen behavior. Once there, she looks him over as I hurriedly explain our mutual disinterest in Hillel House's offerings. Before she can ask too many questions, Daniel and I excuse ourselves and make our way to the garden, where we continue the exchange of information that had begun in his car.

A year from tonight I will be able to explain what merely seems like shyness in this gentle young man sitting at my side under the grape arbor, in the garden that will never be my father's. My mother purchased the house with her husband in mind, the large yard waiting in vain for his return. She had found renters for the small duplex that had just started to feel like home, only to move into a larger house right down the street, close enough to push the piano down the road between one house and the other. A year from tonight I will understand why Daniel's younger brother came to warn me about his sibling, explaining but not clearly enough that his brother is different, that I should be careful; a warning at which I take offense rather than heed. Daniel's long absences without so much as a phone call, and the fact that he hadn't kissed me yet after weeks of on and off dating, will no longer feel like a personal slight, and his dismissal from the U.S. military will become obvious. When I finally discover his whereabouts, the correctional facility's psychiatrist on the other side of the phone will explain that the type of schizophrenia from which Daniel suffers does not appear until early adulthood, and that the two young boys he assaulted while babysitting were lucky to survive. And would I consider writing to him? His family had severed all ties.

Schizophrenia... I hang up the phone and let the word wrap itself around my tongue. I had not heard it for years, not since my girlhood in Israel, when Janek's daughter, Zosha, was an occasional presence in my life. Until the day she attacked my grandmother with a kitchen knife I had not been told she was a possible threat. Withdrawn and sullen during her rare visits to our home, she seemed to reserve a shy smile for me, as if she felt I was safe to be around. I thought she was lovely, her hair falling in soft golden folds around her oval face, her skin almost translucent on her thin arms. Even after the violent outburst was recounted in hushed tones, I still could not believe what the adults were describing; Zosha throwing furniture and clothing off her second floor balcony, down into the street below. The expensive television set her married lover had presented her, exploding into a thousand pieces on the sidewalk. I wasn't sure what was worse, her wanton destruction of property, or the fact that she was involved with a married man. My mother's expression seemed to register an equal amount of disgust at both. I never saw Zosha again.

And now I could add Daniel to the dark corner where Zosha was tucked away, the same corner to which were relegated my childhood memories of the hysterical cleaning lady shrieking so lustily on our bathroom sill. They would keep company as the few people I knew whose fears and madness had shaken themselves free of sanity's restraints, once again leaving me all alone.

*   *   *

Daniel was gone, but like water streaming into a freshly dug hole in the sand, someone else steps right in to take his place. All these months while Daniel was away at Fort Benning trying to be a Marine, his roommate Jack was reading my letters, getting to know me before I even knew he existed. I am surprised the day his first letter arrives; its Georgia address unexpected now that the only military man I know on this side of the world is behind bars. A small photograph falls to the floor as I tear open the envelope, a stern marine face gazing up at me from under a peaked white cap as I bend down to retrieve it. I try to read his face by covering his cap with one thumb, his dress blues with my other, yet the squared jaw and broad nose give back nothing, small eyes staring into the camera with a cold hard look. In his letter Jack explains his relationship to Daniel, asking my permission to correspond, feeling as if he has gotten to know me through the letters he has been reading. My initial feeling of betrayal gives way to curiosity and I decide to reply that same afternoon. Our correspondence continues over the following months, my eagerness growing as I look forward to his tightly filled pages, discussions of literature; dreams for the future, a possible meeting. When the letter with his invitation to join him for a trip to France arrives, the fantasy I had been playing out in my mind takes on a sudden reality I am not certain how to handle. By now he has also revealed that he is divorced, a fact that does not sit well with me, while my mother reacts unexpectedly.

"People make mistakes. You don't know what the reasons may be." And with that she has given me her permission to meet him, a man I have only known through letters in which he addresses me as *Dulcinea* to his *Don Quixote*. How befitting, considering Jack has never spoken to me but through his letters, claiming his love for me from afar. Within weeks all this will change.

* * *

When the plane lands in Dallas I remain seated, gathering my thoughts and nerves as other passengers crowd the aisle. The middle-aged woman that had sat next to me during the nearly four hour flight pats my back as she squeezes past me, eager to disembark. An hour into the flight she had asked where I was headed, and I was almost relieved to have someone to talk to, to say out loud what I was about to do so I could be sure it was really happening.

"How romantic! You've never even met before! It's just like in a movie…" she had chortled, her blue eyes widening behind her rhinestone glasses. Now she turns back and mouths, "Good luck, honey," before giving a little wave and disappearing into the crowd.

But this isn't a movie and the next scene depends on whether I can unglue myself from the seat and make my way down the narrow corridor. The plan is to meet in the airport, then spend one night in Dallas before continuing to France. I had become accustomed to the comfortable back and forth of our letters, Jack's tight flowery script, my confessed dreams and fears, all in the safe realm of narrative time, when I could mull over my words and read and reread his. I didn't even know if I would be able to recognize Jack, my only picture still the passport size square of him in Marine Corps dress uniform, although by now its edges had softened, its paper well-worn from being in my pocket. When the plane has all but emptied, I grip my carry on and smile wanly at the flight attendants thanking me for flying with them today.

The corridor leading from plane to terminal seems shorter than most and all too soon I can see people flanking both sides, waiting for a glimpse of their friends and relatives. I scan the crowd as I keep walking, my eyes searching for a man my heart feels it knows but my eyes fail to recognize. For a brief second my gaze takes in a broad shouldered man with close-cropped hair, his still form covered in a long gray overcoat with upturned collar. He hasn't shifted his position yet his eyes follow me as I pass, and I hesitate only for a moment before I continue past him. The crowd has thinned and I turn back, where the man in the overcoat has now turned and is watching me. I retrace my steps.

"Are you Jack?" He nods, taking a step forward and offering his hand.

"I saw you and you're so pretty I just froze," he says, hazel eyes fixed intently on mine. I don't know how to respond since I've never considered myself pretty despite my mother's biased assurances, finding it difficult believing people who say I am.

"We should head towards the train and find a hotel for tonight. Let me take that." Jack reaches for my suitcase while I follow at his side, amazed that the airport is large enough for a train they call the sky link, to run through it. Within seconds it swoops into the terminal, glass doors slide open and we are inside where he seats himself to my right, close enough for our legs to touch as he bends forward, trying to see my face around the hair I've allowed to partially fall across it, hiding me from his view. Close enough so I can smell the sweet and spicy scent of his cologne. This is the first time he has seen me, not even the advantage of a worn photo in his pocket. And suddenly I am painfully conscious of the outfit I chose for this day, worried that what seemed stylish a few hours ago now appeared juvenile when I so wanted to stop feeling like a child. Neither one of us had ever been at a lack for words in our letters. Face to face we are like actors without our scripts. Yet the need for practical decisions forces us to speak as the train arrives at our stop. Our flight to France is not until tomorrow afternoon, the question I have been afraid to consider hanging in the air between us, and the time has come to face it.

"We need to decide if we're getting one room or two," Jack begins, and I feel like I'm being tested, the future to be determined on how I choose to answer. My mother's voice has followed me to Texas, and I half expect to turn around and find her there waiting for my answer, *the right answer.* Jack must have sensed her presence as well, because he steps a little closer, as if to block her image from my view. This will not be the first time they clash.

"It's your decision, but we're both adults," he says casually. "And we'd be saving some money if we share a room." Good point, I think to myself, as the mental image of my mother tries to squeeze between us the better to glare at me. I quickly push her out of the way suddenly thrilled that Jack hadn't suggested separate rooms. When a college friend back home had asked me what I would do when this moment arrived, I had secretly hoped that this is what Jack would suggest, knowing that I would be disappointed otherwise.

"One room is fine," I say, as I watch his eyes light up mirroring the excitement I feel at this sense of liberation. After arranging for accommodation and calling for the hotel's shuttle, we make our way out into the wintry evening, Jack carrying both his duffel as well as my bag despite my offer to help. Within minutes we are transported away from the airport's bustle, the noise from the bus and our busy thoughts drowning out the need to speak.

In the cold early hours of the next morning, the gray Texas light just starting to filter through the hotel curtains, I might as well have been a lifetime away from the world I had left just the day before. By stepping on to that plane I had entered a different universe, one into which not even my mother could reach. Within hours I was sharing a bed with a man whose written word had charmed me into believing he was the man for me. He had found his soul mate he said, and needed no more time to determine that he was in love and I was the one. I believed him. I had to. This was my chance to walk out of my mother's house and into my own life. Before he turned off the hotel room light at my request, before our bodies joined and consumed each other with a hunger I barely recognized, I had a confession to make. I needed him to know about the abortion, a clean slate before I started the next momentous part of my life.

"My Dulcinea…come here." And he folded me into his arms where I wept as he rocked me back and forth, whispering he loved me no matter what my past contained. I had been held before, but never like this. His grip was like a man hanging on for dear life, a possessive as well as desperate need to protect and control all at once. I would soon learn that there was something primeval in everything he did. The way he made love, ravenously and urgently, as though we were running out of time. The way he ate pizza later on that night, claiming it tasted better when eaten "in bed and naked." The way he held my elbow the next morning, so I would not slip on the icy sidewalk from the hotel to the restaurant where I ordered grits for the first time and the waitress called me sweetie in her southern drawl. The way he eyed other men who merely glanced my way, behavior I first found flattering rather than a sign of worse to come. By the time Air France was tucking its wheels and gaining height, I had agreed to marry him despite his own confession, which he had waited to make after the grits and before the pie arrived, when he could see in my eyes that I was his.

"I need to tell you something... I have two sons who live with their mother in Quebec." He watched me carefully, the same hard unflinching look I had first seen in the picture he sent all those months ago; Eyes that could reach deep inside and read my thoughts. I shuddered to think what they looked like when he was angry. He produced a photo, the faces of two smiling young boys sliding towards me across the linoleum table, undeniable replicas of their father.

Any other woman would have packed herself up and headed home before allowing the earth to fall away thousands of miles beneath her, hurtling towards a foreign country with a virtual stranger. I was silent, thinking only of how secure I felt with him, wanted and protected, sensing something familiar in that barely contained emotion rippling under his surface. The same feeling that had always caused me to want to run, fast, so that whatever was pent up inside could be spent before it exploded. After years of always wondering what would come next, when we would move again, whether I would have friends if we did move, how long they would last when they found out I was only visiting, only temporary, the daughter of a mother with rules no one else had to follow, nothing else mattered but this man across the table from me, waiting for my answer.

"They're beautiful. You could have told me earlier, I would have still said yes." And I meant it. Jack was what came next, this fierce looking man with poetry in his heart and fists always ready to do battle. This man who woke up to run when it was still dark, in Dallas, in Paris, in Tourcoing, where we joined his uncle for Christmas dinner, his aunt trying to warn me to be careful with Jacques, in French I could barely follow. "Il est dangereux..."she said as I tried to make myself useful in her quaint kitchen. I smiled politely, my high school French not enough to explain how her nephew made me feel, lying there in the dark straining to hear his returning footfalls, relief flooding me as I heard his key in the hotel door, felt his weight behind me on the bed when he returned from his predawn excursions. Whatever had haunted him in the night had been left on the pavement he pounded outside, his face now relaxed, his arms around me, safe. With him the world from which I came melted away, chalk on sidewalk after a rain. I had not even called my mother to say I had arrived in France, erasing the life out of which I had just stepped as if I had always been training for this moment; those mad childhood dashes past the hibiscus hedges finally paying off. And even though within days I would begin to see signs of anger in Jack even my love could not tame, I had made my decision. It would take many years until I understood that he had not been the best choice but rather a necessary one. I had been preparing to leave my mother's house for a long time, and Jack provided the opportunity to do so.

* * *

Saying goodbye to Jack frightened me. Saying goodbye in airports always did. Back again in the Dallas terminal, it did not seem possible that we had met only ten days ago, strangers incapable of recognizing each other. Now I could not stop crying, even though he promised to come see me in a couple of weeks when the military allowed him leave. I was not crying only because we had been inseparable for every moment of the nearly two weeks and I could not imagine not having him beside me. I was crying because I would now have to return to that which I had so easily put out of my mind. I had literally written myself out of the exhausting life with my mother who still monitored my every move. A life without a father, who still just drifted in and out when tax time arrived, a silent guest I had given up on trying to enlist in my aid. Now a force greater than what I could conjure was writing me back into the old script, and in just a few hours I would need to explain the ring upon my finger, the one that glistened as the plane took off and sun-rays filtered through the double pane of the window where I hid my tearful face.

*　　*　　*

My mother's reaction to the ring she immediately noticed was what I had expected. She was not pleased.

"What is that?" Her voice was demanding but I had grown bolder in the past few days.

"It's a ring." I knew I was tempting fate but I could not help it. I believed I had found my protector.

"I can see that. Where did you get it?" We both knew the answer to her question but for the script to sound any different I would have had to be someone else's daughter, with a different history.

"Jack gave it to me when he asked me to marry him." A nervous giggle escaped despite my efforts to hold it in. I always laughed when I was anxious.

"And what was your answer?" Another question to which the response she did not want to hear was perfectly obvious.

"I said yes." I turned away, heading down the hall towards my room to unpack, knowing all too well that my mother would follow me, closed doors and privacy never having been part of her policy with her children. She spent the rest of the evening as well as the next days in lecture mode, her lips a perpetual thin line of disapproval, her liberal attitude toward Jack's divorced status forgotten now that he was bringing it closer to home. He was no longer good enough for her daughter and I had not even told her about his sons. Nor was she pleased that he was not Jewish, even though he offered to convert and had already started the process. I could hear her muffled voice on the phone with my father, her tone rising and falling as she complained and cajoled that he do something from his safe distance across the oceans. Yet despite the concern he voiced on the phone with me, he must have known that I had no intention of handing back the ticket with my way out spelled on its front in big bold letters. Who better than my father could understand.

*   *   *

Amazing how rapidly relationships can change; how very different people can be when the stage is set with a new set of props, the scenery altogether foreign from the original against which the characters first met. As long as Jack and I were in France, the two of us wrapped tightly in each other, the outside world could not come in, not into the fairytale we had spun around ourselves and I so wanted to believe. Once back on American soil, I was the little girl being told what to do by her mother, and Jack's aggressive side rose from a low simmer to a pot-rattling boil. His leave had come and gone, not enough time to allow lengthy family discussions and plans for the future. Once his military obligations came to an end and he decided to move to my town so we could be close, reality started to set in. In the few days he spent under our roof in the guest bedroom, we did not have a moment's peace from my mother's suspicious nature. The slightest noise from my room sent her racing down the stairs, bursting through the unlocked door, demanding to know what we had been doing. In between engagement dinner and wedding arrangements, she and Jack clashed on every front, battling over me, over every decision that I, a twenty-three year old woman should have been entitled to make on my own. Instead of finding freedom I had gone from controlling mother to possessive fiancé. From a mother who still determined my curfew to a future husband who put his fists through walls at the slightest provocation.

Once Jack moved into his own apartment, not much changed. While we did have more privacy, my moves were still monitored by phone calls my mother made, demanding when I would be home. And the more of this behavior Jack witnessed the further he appeared to withdraw, disappearing first for hours, then for days, leaving me frantic with worry. His answers were vague when I questioned his whereabouts; the eyes he claimed could read people's very thoughts, not meeting mine. Rather than fight back against my mother's tyranny, he began to react in a tired, defeated sort of way. Like the night I decided to stay in his apartment, talking myself into a confident enough state of mind to stand up to my mother, once and for all. Until the phone call came.

"I need you home; Now." I could picture my mother's lips, a thin tight line, teeth clenched.

"I'm not coming home tonight. I'm staying with Jack." My knees shook but I stood a little taller.

"If you don't come home I'll have your dog put to sleep." And with that she hung up, leaving me foolishly holding the phone, gaping, once more powerless. I decided to call her bluff. Jack thought otherwise.

"Go home. I'll see you tomorrow. You know she's capable of doing this." And with that he saw me to the door where I stood feeling lost, angrier at myself for not standing up to her, than at my mother for being who she had always been. And so the back and forth began as I dutifully ran home to the threats of one then hurried back to bandage the knuckles of the other, once again wishing I could just be like everyone else.

Not Love

California, Winter 1990

"**I**f you leave I might not be here when you come back." A cruel thing to say minutes before I'm whisked away across the oceans to that place that always claims me as its own. How could Jack have known to use this threat above all others, this weapon from the arsenal at his fingertips? But by now there is little of the fairy tale left to tell, our wedding plans set, my better judgment hoarse with screaming out for my attention. My practiced *bonne anne* is stifled in my throat, my rehearsed new year's wish in his dead mother's French, my gift to him for the new year we would not be spending together. There in the airport, my mother hovering in the background, I grip the phone with his voice in my ear, what felt like my lifeline to him, now a heavy anchor dragging me down. "Jack..." I whisper into his ear. And I can hear the quick intake of breath and the distant thudding of his fist against a hard surface, a scene all too familiar and with time more and more difficult to diffuse. I have angered him by agreeing to accompany my mother on a rare visit to my father, a gesture that does not prevent either man from feeling abandoned. Do I recognize the mistake I have made in choosing this man? Yes; down deep in the good sense that I have steadily repressed. Yet I cannot admit that Jack is a stepping-stone, a precarious bridge between the worlds I visit but do not fully inhabit. I recognize the danger he contains but he is also my ticket out. And the more I risk the freer I feel, so I throw myself into loving him the only way I know how, mightily and with an urgency I have learned all too well from the back and forth of my seesaw life. This pressing need to belong, to accept and to be accepted, had blindfolded me that night in a Frankfurt hotel, Jack's wine soaked sorrow at our approaching goodbyes flooding our room with broken glass and blood I hurriedly cleaned up after he had put his elbow through the glass door to the bathroom. I convince myself that his heavy arm draped over me in sleep will keep me safe, ignoring the slight tensing of his fingers if I try to move. I concentrate instead on his beautiful moments. The year's worth of letters written to me before we had even met, addressing me as Dulcinea to his flailing Don Quixote. The kiss we shared on *Monmartre* when the artist captured my face with his inks. The ice cream Jack set out on the windowsill of a Paris hotel to keep in the winter air. The shop into which he disappeared, leaving me under a French moon to wonder until he returned, a delicate ring in hand and a request in his eyes. I stay close but still, while others who do not know him like I do, fear the tell-tale signs of anger on its way, the tightening of a fist, the small muscle in his jaw leaping towards his cheek. I tame it with a finger, smoothing it away until his shoulders relax and the man I want to love returns to his eyes.

And now, once more in an airport where the dramas of my life seem to unfold, my darkest fear has found its way into his words, and for the briefest moment I consider dropping the phone and returning to him, the winter visit to my father abandoned. But I do not. My mother's spell has not yet worn off, the hundred year sleep still draped over her subjects. And by the time my eyes are opened, he will be gone.

Anatomy of Loss

When my mind goes, and it will, I can already feel it slipping away from me on days when the past rolls in like a tide of memories to shore; only my body will remember the losses it has collected. Various parts of me have absorbed the damage done over time, my heart having been dealt most of the blows life doles out as part of its pact with human beings. This heart fissured ever so slightly watching a favorite dog given away when I was six. The fracture widened imperceptibly with each departure from my land and friends. At sixteen it audibly cracked as a boyfriend said a tearful goodbye. And when my father left, this same heart leaped down the airport corridor and threw itself against the heavy metal door behind which I had watched his back walk away from us.

Other losses have collected themselves elsewhere, thoughtfully if deceitfully sparing the heart (it will find out one day). Each time I feel the tears arriving, it is in that space behind my eyelids that the pain announces itself; the hot ripple of that first wave, gathering force and threatening to spill over for the world to see. Like that afternoon, watching Jack drive away from me without a glance back, his love incapable of weathering my mother's interference in our lives. When words cut a little too deep, the ego bruised and slapped once again, it is my palms that accept the punishment of loss, nails digging crescents to weather the brunt of insult. My shoulders help carry the burden, as well. The right one straining under the weight of a grandmother who died before I knew to ask what I now had the courage to voice.

The left one aching beneath a phantom child that should have been cradled there but never saw light. Others' disappointment in me has settled down low in my back. My mother's especially, for allowing that voice to shake itself free and rise up to be heard. Disappointment in myself has selected my ribs, where caged it flutters and flaps every time I fall short of my own expectations.

Each time my body is surprised by a loss it did not see coming, my lungs are the ones to head off the attack like that day when I so eagerly headed towards the old cinema where at age thirteen, I sat in the dark, my hand clasped in the sweaty palm of a boy. I arrived at the lip of a gaping hole where the building once stood, echoes of childhood and the silver screen bouncing off rubble. The startled intake of breath rushed down and crashed into my lungs, as it does each time I discover that change has been permitted while I was away. On mornings when the brain, still muddled with dreams, has to shake itself loose to realize that a loved one is gone, that I'm too late with the bit of news I thought I'd be able to share, such aloneness has to be distributed wherever there is room. Loneliness takes up so much space, waiting to be filled.

The worse loss is yet to come. It constricts the throat and fills my eyes, squeezes my chest, causes me to double over with the impossibility, the sheer ridiculousness of it all being taken away just when I am about to get it right.

Exodus

California, Spring 1991

It may have been the volume of the car radio preventing me from realizing that the screams were coming from my own set of lungs. For a minute I was impressed with their capacity for such sustained noise, and then I started paying attention to the darkening road I was speeding across. I wasn't certain of my destination now that I was free, and since throwing myself out of my mother's house was not in my plans that day, I wasn't prepared for the night ahead. I hadn't left ceremoniously, as other young people in America whose parents prepare for and even anticipate the big day when their children will leave the house. I hadn't left deceitfully either, like my father who kept promising he'd return and then just didn't one day. I exploded out of my mother's house like I had always known I would, my intent loud and clear, pushing past my brother who was dutifully blocking the door with his body, mother's orders, boiling over and searing everything in my path with a fury I hardly recognized. This anger was new and so was the power that came with it. Both feelings arriving as what I had mistaken for love was driving away, his temper and my mother's inability to stay out of our lives ending our brief engagement.

Yet I wasn't ready to enjoy the power, even though its taste was like an aphrodisiac that afternoon when my mother warned I'd burn in hell for behavior of which she did not approve, lapsing into her brief Jesuit past and making me have to remind her that we were Jews. American nights are terribly lonely when you have no one. The first night in a motel was strangely silent as I sat propped against the headboard of the still made bed, watching signs flash their neon heartbeats across the way. I felt temporarily spent after all that screaming which had spilled unbidden from somewhere deep within. Yet going back to my mother's house was not an option, not after the words flung in anger, not after she declared I would no longer be her daughter if I left. I was beginning to understand that no one would save me but myself, my father having chosen a life far from us, and no gallant knight on the darkening horizon. The next night was spent in my car, parked on a side road out of the lamplight's reach, plunged in a darkness punctuated by passing headlights of cars that grew fewer as the night progressed. Israeli nights are filled with sound, neighbors washing dishes, arguing over the evening news, coming over uninvited for a cup of coffee and the latest gossip. Here the silence takes getting used to, and the absence of my country's sounds weighed heavily at first. I could have died in my sleep, and no one would have bothered until the rent was late. I had moved into a small apartment, locked the door and closed the blinds tight behind me. Money was scarce yet I sent my brother away when he showed up with care packages from my still silent mother. "Don't need your charity or your pity," I declared. And night after night I filled the tub with water hot enough to scorch, to remind myself I was alive, sank up to my nose in its enveloping heat and began to drink. I drank in anger at my father, for leaving me with his wife to navigate through a country in which I still felt like a guest. He had claimed Israel for his own, never asked if here is where I wanted to be, merely assumed that I, like my mother, chose to leave him behind. I drank out of sorrow, missing the friend who would never have allowed me to feel this alone had she been on the same side of the world. I drank because I was certain no man would ever touch me again and I ached to be held.

My self-pity was so immense it filled my every fiber until there was no room to allow for hope to sneak in.

And then one evening comes a knock on the door. A quick look out the peephole to ensure that it isn't my brother sent on yet another mission reveals nothing but a dark form, too large to be family. I open without asking the form to identify itself, part of the recklessness I have adopted as my new way of life. The same recklessness that sends me driving too fast every night, windows rolled down, music so loud I can feel it in my blood, wind slapping against my outstretched hand catching the silky strands of dark; A heedlessness that sends me to the apartment pool to swim away my insomnia, until my legs are shaky and almost too weak to carry me back to my bed where I hope for dreamless torpor. There in the doorway stands a man, dark, unshaven, unsmiling, a wide plate of steaming food balanced on one large palm of his outstretched arm. "Look like you could use some meat on those bones," is all he says before he turns on his heel and walks back down the hall. I feel the heat of the food through the heavy plate and I whisper a thank you after his retreating back. At the small table at which I never sit, I take in the bounty a stranger has cooked for me. Red rice, refried beans, meat finely shredded and arranged against floury tortillas. I sink into the single chair and breathe in more than the spices used to make this simple meal. I breathe in the welcome and the kindness he must have rolled into the dough when he included me in his thoughts tonight. I cry into my plate then eat better than I had in weeks. And then I sleep.

Running Away

California, Winter 1991

I was not planning on returning and the suitcase alone was proof of that. The white haired driver at the Sacramento terminal knew this when he offered to help me lift it into the belly of the idling greyhound bus, his lighthearted "You got rocks in here?" followed by a more serious glance when I did not respond. The young man who slid into the seat next to me had known as well, his long limbs spilling into the aisle, his boots as dusty and worn as the cowboy hat perched on the mop of his dirty blond hair. "Running away?" He asked, gray eyes taking in my thin frame with a measured look. By the time the Cascades loomed ahead, framed in the large front windows of the lumbering bus, he had heard about the man I was supposed to marry but did not, about my plan to prove that I was no longer under my mother's spell by following him to Canada in the dead of winter, where he had escaped from the craziness my mother created around her. I told him about the ring I was carrying deep in the pocket of my coat, the promised future it once held weighing me down with its loss. At a forlorn station on the Canadian border, he excused himself before unfolding his tall frame and braving the winter cold for a quick smoke, returning with the smell of snow and a steaming cup of cocoa he bought just for me, concern for my worsening cough registering in his eyes.

"He shouldn't have let you travel by yourself," he commented before tipping his hat over his eyes, his chin on his chest for a quick nap.

"He doesn't know I'm coming" I replied, causing one cowboy eye to open in surprise before he settled back into the raised collar of his coat.

The bus ride back was lonely, nothing but tangled thoughts crowding my mind and overflowing into the empty seat to my left. The now lighter suitcase was no longer cause for amusement, most of its contents left in a Canadian hotel room as proof that I had existed for the man who had not changed his mind about making me his wife. My hand lay fisted around empty space in my coat pocket, the box with its ring left on the hotel dresser where Jack avoided it until I turned away. His eyes no longer looked at me with the love they had held such a short time ago. I might as well have been a stranger, his stare as cold as it had been in the military photo where I had first seen his face, when so much promise had still stretched between us.

The cowboy was right about one thing I thought, my forehead pressed against the cold window trying to stop myself from replaying the sadness of the last two days. I deserved better than this.

*   *   *

The apartment was dark and cold as I let myself in on the evening of my return. I had not been gone long and still, the air in the room contained a deep loneliness as of a place abandoned for some time. The ringing of the phone shattered the silence, making me jump. Few people had my number, my mother not counted among them, which is why her voice on the other end of the line was unexpected and surprisingly timed.

"Your co-worker, Ann gave me your number. You could have told your mother where you were going." After months of silence between us this was how she started a conversation. Ann was the middle-aged preschool teacher with whom I worked at the private Jewish school in the next town. I had made her promise not to tell anyone where I was headed unless there was a family emergency and someone's life was at stake; then and only then could she give out information. This phone call meant that someone had better be dying.

"Are you listening to me?" Her voice was needling, my muscles tensing at the sound. "I need you to come home. We have to talk." I couldn't imagine what was still left to talk about. I was tired, a deep exhaustion that tugged at me like a child at its parent's sleeve. The last thing I needed was to sit through interminable lectures by my mother.

"I'm not coming home. Whatever you need to say you can tell me over the phone." My attempt at leaving her far behind may have failed physically, but emotionally I could feel the distance frosting over my voice. Home. I couldn't begin to explain how confusing the word had become. I looked at the bare walls of the drab apartment, the narrow adjoining bedroom where I cried myself to sleep and awoke almost disappointed that I had to face another day. This was not where I was supposed to be yet it was better than my mother's house where not a corner existed in which her voice didn't follow, where I always felt on the verge of suffocation.

"Your father is ill and I need you to fly to Israel to be with him. You'll have to come here to get your passport and the ticket I bought." When I had considered emergencies my father had not been part of the possible scenarios. He was a figure I had learned to put out of my mind. A wraith-like entity that floated into our lives once a year to help do the taxes, part of my mother's grand future plans while she, and as a result her children, lived without him. He was part of that place I used to call home.

"You're his wife. Why aren't you going?" The question seemed logical to me. Wives took care of sick husbands. They didn't leave them alone for years, putting marriages on hold, sending daughters to check on them in their stead.

"Aunt Stefa died while you were chasing Jack. I'm going to Spain to meet your grandmother. I need to be with her since I couldn't make it to Israel to aunt Stefa's funeral and we're meeting half way. It's already arranged and your flight leaves tomorrow." So someone *had* died while I was following my heart. My grandmother's older sister whose garden I would now never see again, her lemon tree perfuming its farthest reaches with an intoxicating scent I could almost smell as I stood, eyes closed in the middle of my miserable apartment. Once again my mother was arranging my life, pulling the strings to which I was still if reluctantly attached. And what amazed me more than the decision she had made without asking me, was her choice to spend time with her mother rather than fly to my father's side. Now she was expecting the same misplaced loyalty from her own daughter.

"What's wrong with dad?" I needed to know what to expect, unsure about my mother's motives. If he was seriously ill she should be the one going and if not then this was just a ruse to get me away from my latest addiction. My mother was attempting to save me again.

"Something with his kidneys, he wouldn't tell me. But he could use your help." There wasn't the slightest hint of concern in her voice, in fact she sounded almost doubtful that he was sick at all. She was sending me to be her eyes, and if she could distance me from Jack at the same time, even better.

*   *   *

El Al flight sixty-seven landed in Tel Aviv to the usual enthusiastic applause from passengers grateful to be home. There it was again. That word I had such trouble defining. I held back my own applause, unsure what I felt at finding myself back on Israeli soil without the much talked about fiancé in tow. A gray sky and a light breeze met me at the top of the metal staircase leading down to the tarmac. I had exchanged one winter for another.

I had not seen my father since his visit to the States the previous summer, and by the time my mother's phone call had found me enough time had passed for him to regain his health and stand at the arrival gate waiting for me, a bit grayer at the temples, his frame thinner than I remembered. I could not recall how long it had been since the two of us were alone. No younger brother vying for his attention. No wife telling him what to say to make me mind her. After a brief flurry of catching up conversation we drove in silence through the wintry evening, the slightly lowered windows creating a mournful whistling as I watched the familiar landscape of the place I still loved. There was an awkward silence, both of us avoiding the painful subject of the cancelled wedding, my bus ride to Canada, and my glaring weight loss. My father had indeed been very ill, and tests had shown what doctors suspected to be a tumor near his kidneys. Fortunately, this had not been the case, and instead the problem turned out to be a birth defect that had gone undetected. Years later he would joke that my mother would have been very happy to be his widow, knowing all too well that his wife enjoyed the prestige associated with being married to a university professor, but not the intimacies of marriage itself.

Minutes before taking the turn that would bring me back to the neighborhood of my youth, my father broke the silence, his voice unsure as though he'd been deciding how to broach a difficult subject. His casual tone seemed forced, yet I attributed it to nothing more than being unaccustomed to speaking with someone who was more a stranger than a daughter.

"When we get home a colleague of mine will be waiting in

the house to meet you. She used to be my teaching assistant. Her name is Daniela." Looking back years later I find it astounding that I had been so naïve as to simply accept his explanation without question. Despite the strangeness of my parents' long distance marriage, my mother's stubborn insistence that we were the perfect family had seeped into my belief system, preventing me from seeing what was there before my eyes. I climbed the stairs to the living room of the house on *Narkisim* like a sleep walker climbing back into a dream, back into my childhood home where nothing seemed to have changed other than the henna-haired woman standing where my mother should have been. She seemed pleasant enough, a mixture of curiosity and hesitation in her eyes as she sat watching me while I took stock of my surroundings. The old piano sat mutely against the far wall, hours of practice swallowed in its wooden depths. The same two boys sat frozen in the painting hanging in the dining room, their mouths wide open in anticipation of the grapes their hands held eternally suspended above their heads. And the rectangular gas heater still growled to life as my father bent over it with a match, braving the flaming tongue that leapt out as threatening as always.

Daniela seemed quite comfortable in these familiar surroundings, and had I not suffered from a combination of jet lag and naiveté I may have paid closer attention to the ease with which she treated my father, as well as her knowledge of where items were kept in my mother's kitchen. After a cup of tea she offered to prepare and a brief conversation, she excused herself for the evening, arranging to meet me the next morning while my father attended to his work. And I followed my feet as they led me up the familiar tile steps to my childhood room, where time had stood still while I wandered away, returning with a broken heart.

*   *   *

The next ten days of the visit to my father proved to be just what the doctor ordered, and had I not continued suffering from an entirely too trusting heart, I would have done the math and realized that my mother had sent me knowing that Daniela was a therapist. My father went along with the idea, both parents concerned that I would still attempt to bring Jack back into my life. My mother's instructions to Daniela through my father were to treat me in her capacity as a psychotherapist, to get Jack out of my system, as though my heart, like her husband, could be ordered what to do.

What I actually needed was someone who would let me talk while all they did was listened. And Daniela turned out to be the sounding board I sorely lacked. My mother had never been my confidante, her puritan beliefs and rigid upbringing an impossible outlet for the conversations I ached to have. I soon discovered that Daniela hadn't stumbled into therapy for nothing. She had an uncanny ability to understand what I was experiencing before I could even phrase it in the language that no longer came as easily as it once did. Morning after morning as we shopped, sat in coffee houses and indulged in chocolates, I could feel that I was returning to myself, reveling in the freedom I was allowed to unburden my heart. She was a generous listener, hearing me without judging and with absolutely no intention of following my mother's wishes. So while the time we spent together may have proved to be therapeutic, what I ended up walking away with was a friend. She also understood that my evenings belonged to my father, excusing herself to return to her own family while my father and I became reacquainted.

The strangeness of having my father to myself soon wore off, as we fell into a comfortable routine of sharing quiet dinners and evenings once he returned home from work. Unlike my mother around whom drama exploded and filled our lives with tension, my father was content to sit with a book, music playing quietly in the background. We were not accustomed to lengthy conversations. Our interaction was usually reserved for questions I used to have regarding homework, and books we both loved and my father was always happy to discuss. The occasional letter he would send addressed to me alone would more often than not contain a Xeroxed copy of a story he wanted me to read, a note attached in his elegant hand simply reading, "I thought you'd like this. Love, Dad." We were the literary version of American fathers connecting with their sons by having a catch. During this visit I came to expect his footfall on the stairs before he went to bed, on his way to say goodnight to the daughter who had been briefly restored to his life. Not having been included in my parents' plans, I had never given any thought to whether my father was happy to be left alone in this old house for so many years. The pain of his brief, guest-like visits had dulled over time, and so it was with some surprise that I once again saw him as a being with feelings that my mother rarely took into consideration. Yet there he stood one night, leaning against the doorframe of my room, watching as I sat brushing my hair.

"Did you need anything, dad?" The hint of a smile hovered over his face, his eyes staring with a mixture of sadness and concentration that was beginning to make me uncomfortable.

"No, just looking at you. Sleep well." No further explanation was offered, and none was demanded. If there were anything my father wanted to tell me, he would find a way.

*   *   *

My visit to my father soon came to an end, and I had managed to avoid both friends and most of my family, a brief visit to my grandmother before she left for Spain to meet with my mother as familial as I was capable of being this time around. I even made excuses when Ronit discovered I was home, unable to bear the idea of repeating my sad story one more time, then seeing the pity in her face. My life seemed charmed to the friends I'd left behind in this country. "Lucky girl, flying off to America all the time," they would say, while they had to stay, waking up to the same story every day. How could I explain that all I wanted now was to wake up in one of their scripts, in one of the apartments I could see out my window, solid, down to earth structures in which my friends slept in the arms of solid, down to earth men. I just wanted to forget, to go to sleep one night and wake up only to find out that it had all been a bad dream. Jack would be waiting in the airport in California, and I would be his *Dulcinea* once again. Instead, the morning of my flight arrived, my eyes opening to the familiar darkness of my old room, and one lone suitcase packed and ready to go by the front door.

I said my goodbyes to Daniela the day before, one last heart to heart over coffees before I returned to the loneliness from which I had been temporarily relieved. I had enjoyed my time with her, feeling comfortable in her presence almost immediately. She allowed me to be myself even when I wasn't so sure who that self was just yet, meeting me when I was still hovering between my need for independence and my search for someone who would take care of me; Between my desire to be considered an American woman, and my immigrant habit of looking back at what could have been had I stayed in Israel; Daniela listened to what I had to say, giving weight to my words and keeping me from floating away, like I always felt I would when my words failed and I was not being heard. She held me tightly minutes before I turned to leave, surprising me when I saw tears brimming in her eyes. She too like my father seemed loaded with a story I did not know how to read.

Meeting My Future

California, Spring 1992

When his sister-in-law suggested she introduce us, I nodded politely, my escape to Canada already in the workings, the idea of ever loving another man a ridiculous impossibility. I could not imagine starting my story all over again for a complete stranger. Yet I had nothing to lose by agreeing to meet this man everyone referred to as Uncle Mark, since I was not planning on returning, certain that finding me on his doorstep would rekindle Jack's love for me. I had been wrong.

When I returned from the visit to my father and was introduced to Mark I attempted to maintain a disinterested attitude. After all, too many men had failed me, and I was getting used to the idea of being on my own. As lonely as I felt, I was learning to deal with the world without being responsible for anyone but myself, not answering to a mother's or a boyfriend's demands to be someone I was not. Yet it was becoming increasingly difficult to resist the charms of the man who came to collect his nephew from my preschool class every afternoon. There was simplicity to him that I found refreshing; an air of calmness that I had forgotten was possible after the intensity of Jack's mood swings. Mark didn't seem to expect anything, his behavior motivated by nothing other than his good nature. He retrieved a lost shoe when a parent hadn't noticed it had fallen out of a stroller. He came along on a fieldtrip to the zoo, opening juice boxes, giving piggyback rides, and answering knock-knock jokes with unflagging patience. And he made me laugh, something I hadn't done in a very long time. When Mark finally worked up the courage to ask me out he scribbled my phone number in crayon on a scrap of paper, seated on a miniature chair after snack time at the preschool. *Strong hands,* I silently observed, watching his firm hold around the small red crayon. *Oh no,* I heard somewhere behind the ramparts recently built around my heart, promising myself I wouldn't fall for this again. But the children gravitated towards him in a show of trust I could not help but notice, sensing a kindness I would find most endearing as our time together progressed.

Even after we started dating I kept waiting for something to go wrong. When we missed an exit on the road I watched Mark's face for signs of anger that never arrived, surprised instead by his suggestion that we see where the road take us. When he hurt his knee badly enough one evening to require medical attention, I waited for his impatience with the emergency room staff, only to find them in stitches over a joke he made while I was briefly out of the room. And after a night of lovemaking in the small apartment we now shared, I woke up to find him propped up on one elbow watching me sleep. No heavy arm pinning me possessively, a smile at his good fortune playing on his lips.

When a year elapsed and he had not left, despite my mother whom he eventually had to meet, ("My grandparents were like that" his only comment after an afternoon in her company,) I stopped waiting for something terrible to take it all away. For months I had waited for Mark to leave and not come back, kissing him at the door to our apartment each time he left for work as if for the very last time. I would watch him walk out, my eyes following from the window as he drove away, panic gripping my heart at the thought of what life would be like if he did not return. Those lonely nights and depressingly long days seemed like someone else's story by now, and I could not imagine living them again. And when I allowed myself to think of it, the sheer coincidence of having met considering the vast ground I had covered over the years of our traveling, and the handful of men I had nearly given myself over to out of my need to escape my mother's oppressive grip, terrified me. Had my family stayed in one place, had my father accepted teaching assignments anywhere else in the world (he had been offered one in Kalamazoo and one in Edinburg), our paths may have never crossed. And once I discovered that Mark's older brother had attended university in Davis where we had lived off and on over the years, I could not help but wonder whether we may have passed each other on the street on his visits to his sibling, quickly doing the math and finding that there was one year during which we were actually there at the same time. I could not imagine that he would have given me a second glance considering the difference in our ages. I in pigtails and still playing with dolls while he was already dating and living on his own.

I had to start believing that I was worth staying around for, and that it would take more than an intrusive mother to cause Mark to leave. And even though Jack left me after he had put a ring on my finger and had driven off with a car full of our future kitchen items, wedding invitations barely dry on the printer's desk, I had to find a way to place my faith in this kind-hearted man whose calm demeanor could not possibly have hidden any dark secrets. I would have to learn to trust again, starting by letting him answer the phone in our apartment, no longer worried that my mother would discover that we were living together.

After weeks of warning me that he would ask me to marry him, one day he actually did, right there on the tattered sofa where we talked our nights away. And after I stopped laughing, realizing the question was serious this time, the man having asked it uncommonly solemn as well for a change, there was no hesitation before I accepted his proposal. "You'll have to ask me too," he added, earnest about this request, as well. And a few days later I did just that, giggling like a school-girl as I explained my task to the bewildered florist writing down my message before delivering my proposal and a bouquet to the school where Mark worked. His proposal was not a claiming of property based on a whimsical literary fantasy. No Don Quixote flailing at imaginary windmills this time. Mark was giving me an integral role in the decision making, allowing me to feel the weight of a responsibility that would affect us both for the rest of our lives together. This time my mind agreed with my heart that this was the right decision to make. I was not saying yes to escape my mother's house. I had already done that. I was saying yes because I found what I had always longed to have; the tranquility and confidence of what I considered a normal relationship, with a man who woke up with a smile on his face and went through life without expecting to do battle at every turn. With Mark there was no drama, no tension. While I had once been enamored with the danger other men contained, I now welcomed the mystery of Mark's calmness. All of a sudden my miserable apartment was not miserable any more. The battered sofa I had talked the manager into letting me have despite a rental agreement that did not include furniture, became the comfortable setting for hours of conversation during which Mark and I slowly revealed our histories. The cheap linoleum topped dining table transformed into the location for many romantic dinners despite my meager culinary skills. And the narrow bed in which I had cried myself to sleep invited us both to hungrily explore, the only sense of urgency this time in my need to make up for lost time. The blinds that I had kept shut for so many months were opened wide to invite the world in to share in my joy. After years of wondering what I was doing in a country where I had felt so alone for so long, the thought of being in America made me happy again, like it had all those years ago, our suitcases waiting by the door, the smell of adventure in the air.

Lying in bed, Mark asked me once long ago when we were still learning each other by touch, to describe how he made me feel, still needing affirmation. "You're the writer," he said. "Use your words," his face bent over mine expecting greatness. But no words came despite the music filling my veins at the mere sensation of his body beside mine. And I could see the shadow of disappointment crossing his face, doubting my love because I couldn't turn it into clever phrases. I couldn't tell him, not then, that what he had awakened in me was larger than words, an entity filling my lungs with much needed air. A resurrection only someone who had almost drowned could understand.

One day the words would come, and I now believed he would still be there to hear them.

California, Fall 1992

My father waited until after our engagement party to announce that he was leaving my mother. It appeared that he wanted to see his daughter out of the house and taken care of before making his decision public, despite the obvious tension with which such a declaration tinted the wedding atmosphere. While I had been witness to my parents' less than idyllic marriage, the possibility that they would not stay together had never entered my thoughts. That they had been living in separate countries for the past five years was simply part of my mother's plan, odd but not open to discussion. Other marriages fell apart, especially among the American families we knew, whose households consisted of arrangements as far removed from their original configuration as imaginable. Not in our family.

My initial reaction was a tremendous sadness, an inability to understand that what my father had done, while poorly timed, had to happen for his own sanity. My mother's response was complete surprise and outrage followed by denial. This was yet another challenge for her to overcome, one more opportunity to show strength of character. And of course, her children were expected to be loyal to the mother and wife who had done no wrong, by joining what soon became a campaign to save my father from "*that woman.*" Yet no amount of pleading, discussing or threatening swayed my father from the decision he had taken most of his unhappy married life to make. The notion of loyalty had been drilled into me for years, and I was now expected to demonstrate it by taking my mother's side without question. But no questions meant not finding out the truth, and once we were told who the other woman actually was, the anger I felt demanded an explanation.

"Daniela." My father's mouth had formed the letters of her name, but when they came out my heart would not allow the sounds to add up. How was this possible? And how could I not have known? I thought back to my winter visit, the relief I felt as I unburdened my heart to a woman who had seemed so sincere. Suddenly I felt like such a fool at having been lied to, for not reading all the signs that had been right there, in my father's sad eyes, in Daniela's tearful goodbye. My father had wanted us to meet, hoping to create a connection between his child and the woman he saw as his future wife before I had a reason to hate them both. Conflicting emotions were running riot in my mind. I regarded that handful of days spent with my father as a gift, a connection I had sorely missed to both him and the country I still longed for in my dreams. I felt betrayed by a woman I had come to consider a friend, regretting having allowed myself to speak intimately, feeling as though I had tipped myself over and spilled contents I could never gather back. The sensation that I might float away in the confusion of it all, returned. The difference now was that I had Mark whose kind eyes looked at me as if he had known me even before he knew me, pulling me back down to earth and into his shoulder where I could howl my pain.

Saying Goodbye to Houses

Israel, December 1992

Maybe this time I'll walk a little further into the courtyard and show Mark where I came from. I'll bring him to the street where I grew up, to the house to which I didn't get to say goodbye before divorce proceedings began. I will stand on the sidewalk and watch him walk away from me down the narrow alley between the buildings, curious to see his future bride's past. He will come back, (I would eventually get used to that,) smiling no less, describing what he had seen until I ask him to stop, since it will sound like too many changes were made to the home that used to be mine.

This time I'll hold his hand and lead him past the hibiscus hedges, *watch for bees*, beyond the garbage bins, *hold your breath*, under the neighbors' laundry lines, *watch the dripping*, and into the courtyard where nothing will have changed. Beyond the heavy armored door, patients will be waiting to see my father, listless housewives, angry husbands, troubled teenagers. *Don't stare.* Mark will follow me up the carpeted staircase and into the sun-filled living room where soft classical music will be playing until we're called for dinner. The dining room windows will be thrown open, the smell of Shabbat dinners drifting above the courtyard, fanned by the light flutter of bats nesting in the fruit trees below. He won't be allowed in my room because mother says it isn't proper. We'll be seated on black wrought iron chairs with red velvety seats, all except that one with the burn mark on its cushion from the time the dog ran away and the nervous cook set down the simmering pot. *Don't ask you'll never hear the end of it.* Father will be seated at the head of the table, his back to the curious neighbors in the apartments across the way. They will already have noticed that I brought home a young man, and by now the news will have traveled down the street, caught on the evening breeze.

Mother will watch to see if Mark has been taught proper dinner table etiquette, not that strange habit Americans have, silverware any which way and one hand under the table. After dinner I'll ask for permission to go for a walk and Mark will have to promise to bring me back before dark. We'll walk down the street where I grew up, past the prying eyes of neighbors, my hand held warmly in his, all the way to the Pitango tree with its red bitter fruit, winding our way down the alley where boys always tried to steal kisses in the shadowy darkness of concrete walls. Yet first I will sneak him upstairs to my room, to see the fairy tale world I used to live in. Childhood posters on the turquoise walls, glass cabinets trapping souvenirs, lacy curtains at the window through which I watched, waiting for the idea of him.

But wait. We're too late. By the time Mark arrives, mother is gone, across the seas to her second home. The house on *Narkisim* Street in which part of me is embedded in every corner, stands dismantled, furniture, toys, dishes, all sold or given away, my memories still attached. Those neighbors who used to report my every move, kept silent as they watched that other woman come and go, a key to my past in her hand.

Wedding Day

Israel, April 1993

The photographs captured it all, from the tension in the air to the strained smiles on guests' faces. If not for the billowing white dress I had carried across the oceans and now awkwardly wore, and the *chupa*, the wedding canopy perched on the small stage at the back of the hall, I would have been easily convinced I'd walked into the middle of a wake.

I always knew the man I would marry would not be from this land; Israeli men with their easy, confident ways, whether *Ashkenazi* or *Sephardic*, just hadn't felt right. The former seemed to think they knew it all, and wanted the world to know they did. The latter were too macho for their own good, sporting mentalities that would have kept me on a restrictive leash I would have quickly resented. Both brands of arrogance would never have worked. I needed someone who would understand where I came from but didn't hail from there himself and something deep inside me knew it. That same something that had chosen this unassuming bearded man now seated at a distant table, wedged between my father who was translating, and the rabbi who was instructing this American beside him. Had I not been so preoccupied I would have felt sorry for the startled look on his sweet face, a cross between panic and bewilderment at what he had gotten himself into.

Lesser men would have fled. It wasn't enough that I had dragged Mark across the world to be married in the Middle East of all places. A world that no longer alarmed me with its brash, pushy attitude, but a place bound to take newcomers by surprise. And it didn't wait long to do so. It assailed with its first hot humid breath as you stepped out of the plane, and continued the baptism by immersing new members in a world of honking cars, armed civilians, raucous street vendors, abrasive language. I had introduced this polite American suburbanite into my old world, and I was doing so in the midst of one of the most unpleasant battles waged on this already bloodied soil, the battle between my parents who had decided to dissolve their marriage just as we were beginning our own. Any semblance of civility between the two had been abandoned, as my naturally dramatic mother openly raged, while my no longer silent father retaliated.

We did the only logical thing we could. We ran away. Each morning as lines were drawn and the skirmish began, we hurried down the stairs from my childhood room where we'd kept safe in each other's arms, and out the front door, my mother's "I'll make you pay for this," and my father's "You already have!" ricocheting over our heads as we ran for safety. It didn't matter where. The decision could be made on the bus, its long ride into the city our chance to catch our breath and calm jangled nerves. The wedding preparations were not in our hands anyway, since during breaks from severing their own ties, my parents were busy arranging for ours. By the time Haifa's buildings loomed ahead we were ready to face the day, exploring hand in hand, incredulous at our narrow escape from the battlefield and at the love that seemed to shield us.

Yet here we were in the hall rented for the occasion, one of the last times we would all gather under the same roof pretending to be family. My mother looked gaunt, her emerald colored dress hanging off her thin shoulders. My father stood in dark suit and tie, his hands crossed behind his back as if standing at attention. Both still wore their wedding rings, as if a truce had been temporarily called until the festivities were over. Both posed for photographs, my mother's arm casually looped through my father's as though in wedded bliss. I moved between well-wishers in a daze, my two worlds colliding and sizing each other up. The woman who would within moments become my mother-in-law shared the same startled look as her son who was now being led to the wedding canopy by my father and Janek. Old neighbors and friends appraised my choice of husband in sidelong glances I kept trying to decipher. Soon I too was walked across the red carpet leading to my future, the symbolic transition from parents' home to a husband's. There I stood grasping the hand of a man now promising to cherish me forever as my father leaned in to explain what he was being told to say by the rabbi. Ludicrous, I thought to myself, wondering what my father could be thinking as he watched this stranger place a shiny gold band on my finger. I tried hard not to catch my best friend's eye, afraid my nerves would betray me, and I'd let out the loud guffaw working its way up my throat.

What I didn't know at that moment could have changed the heaviness I had been carrying as if it sat, right there on the lengthy pearled train of that ridiculous dress. That weight I dragged the seven customary circles around the wedding canopy, avoiding my father's eyes each time around. Seven circuits representing the sevenfold bond marriage would create between bride and groom and their families. Seven earthly rotations symbolizing the days it took to create the world. Did the rabbi know that while I saw the last turn around the canopy as the bond connecting me to the man I was encircling, my father was probably counting down the minutes left until he could untie his own? And then came the reading of the *ktuba*, the marriage contract, in which the groom pledges to provide, honor, and support in truth; that same contract over which my parents were now waging war.

After three attempts the glass broke under Mark's nervous foot; and just like that, we belonged to each other. I still didn't know what years later the pictures so clearly told. The lost look in my father's eyes, the anguish of a man who had suffered silently for years, waiting until he saw me taken care of before he walked away. The photograph of the four of us, my father looking towards the camera his gaze already beyond it, then me, my back slightly turned towards him, just enough to pretend he wasn't there. Two silent years would have to elapse before he would share his truth with me and I would allow him back into my life. Next in the photo is my husband of ten minutes with my mother to his left, the kindness with which he would continue to amaze me already there in the hand he's clasping around my mother's for support. The picture of my grandmother, her beautiful hands already twisted in the unforgiving illness that would soon trap her within her own body. Even she had kept secrets from me, my father telling me long after she was gone, that she'd said only a crazy Hungarian like him would have lasted that long with her crazy daughter. Standing at my grandmother's side is her husband Janek, posing as usual in profile, his eyes sunken, his face pale, the last time I will see him before his death in a year.

I don't know any of this as I walk from table to table greeting guests, figuring that if I keep moving I'll be able to dodge my father who is bound to want to say something to his newly married daughter. I'm too hurt to hear what he has to say, too wrapped up in my own fears to accept that he is finally facing his. Most guests are aware of the circumstances, my father's side of the family sitting at their assigned table in formal silence. And when the dancing begins, I watch as my parents grimly hold each other's hands, my father's arm reluctantly placed on my mother's back as she weakly smiles at the intruding lens. An old family friend insists on making this evening joyous, despite the tension stretched taut across the hall, like tripwires ready to explode under our feet. She leads the guests in dance, then gathers men to lift bride and groom on chairs where high above the crowd, we exchange a brief private look before we're brought back down to earth. Had I known more truths that day, I would have embraced the moment rather than cringed from it. The last photograph in our wedding album would have been different. Not my father sadly smiling, my hand in his, my face averted from the man who had yet to tell me his version of the story. I wouldn't have made the call earlier that day, warning Daniela to stay away from us tonight, afraid she'd show up and make matters worse.

In a few days we would get back on that plane, leave this world and the people who had come to celebrate us behind, until distance and experience would allow the lens of time to focus on the truths, sending us back to make amends.

Scents

I f you ask me to recall the exact dates of my many visits to either one of my countries, I won't be able to answer, not right away. We packed and unpacked our lives so many times, in so many places, that after awhile they all became muddled, and distinguishing one visit from the other by time and year was no longer possible for me. What I could tell you though, is the way certain moments and places in my life smelled. Like the house we rented on Hermoza lane in California one summer, the last house on the block before the stretch of fields. The open windows brought in the sweet yellow scent of golden wheat, swaying like waves in the summer breeze. I don't know what the place smelled like in any other season, since we moved to a more permanent location by the time fall arrived.

Schools I attended had distinct smells as well. You knew you were in an Israeli school yard at snack time when the air became permeated with the flowery scent of tangerines, children peeling open the orange globes, fingers stained yellow from the sweet juice. I couldn't tell you much of what I learned in a Californian ninth grade science class, but what marks my unremarkable time in that room, is the colorfully perfumed presence of the girl who sat next to me. She was large. Her black wavy hair formed clouds around her freckled face, and a dimpled chin hovered just above enormous sweaters with wide collars that dipped towards her ample chest. I noticed her chest because I didn't have one yet. She smelled purple, more than likely because she chewed grape flavored gum with which she blew tremendous lavender bubbles right there in class, before the teacher's eyes. California always smelled purple after that.

Certain moments overwhelm me with undated yet vivid memories, like the afternoon when I wandered into my daughter's room to change the bedding, and right there in the crisp snap of the fresh sheets, hid the unmistakable scent of my grandmother's apartment. The woman had been dead for a year, her apartment sold long before that, yet there she was, on the wrong side of the world, the satin smell of her cigarettes and perfume an entity, as if I could turn and find her there behind me. The ocean breeze from her Haifa apartment nestled in my daughter's linen, waiting to be resurrected. I could almost hear her sharp knife slicing through fresh cucumbers, preparing breakfast in her tiny kitchen. I must have snapped those sheets a half dozen times, making them billow into the air then watching them fall gently back onto the bed below, until my wrists tired and my lungs were incapable of inhaling deeply any longer. I'd had to let her go.

Some of my favorite places and people must have known that I would leave them behind one day, since their presence seems to have traveled with me, summoned like spirits at a séance, hazy and drifting just within my reach. One arrived yesterday afternoon, in a small cardboard box containing a forgotten pair of reading glasses. They had been found in the car my father had rented during his last visit to me. Lifting out the soft brown case, I brought it to my nose, a habit that has served me well, breathing in a mixture of worn leather and fading aftershave. Then sliding out the thin metal frames, I perched them on my nose, my world slipping out of focus for the briefest of moments. And there he was, my father, conjured up for one heartbeat instant before I placed his glasses back in their case, and into the box in which they had been sent, trapping the memory smell to be savored another day.

I travel this way as I busy myself about my daily tasks. These unexpected gifts my past bestows come in the most ordinary of packages. I lower my face into an old book I dust off, and there around me is the school library of my childhood, where classmates raced each other to be the first to grab one of only two copies of an assigned book. I pass a stranger's house during an evening stroll, and stand rooted to the spot as the smell of frying onions wafts out onto the street. It carries with it dizzying images of Israeli women preparing family dinners in a country where fast food had still been in its infancy when I was a child. I walk down a city street and as I turn the corner, drifting around the bend to meet me is the smell of my old neighborhood after a rain. If I just look up I might catch a glimpse of a familiar face in an open window. But I know better than to try, since part of me realizes these are mere illusions, a momentary merging of two worlds neither one of which my heart is willing to let go. Yet practicing the magic of conjuring them up is a dangerous game, one in which I could lose myself, slip under and forget to come up for air.

Phone Calls

California, 1999

It is almost time to make the call, one of only two we allow ourselves each year. I sit on my porch under a dark California sky, smelling the night air of a now familiar land. Sweet hay from the meadows across town, and the perfumed scent of jasmine from the white flowers I now anticipate every spring, each one a perfect little pinwheel of snowy petals. The phone sits on the step by my side, the address book propped on my lap because once a year isn't enough to remember such a long number. Country code is followed by city code, then Ronit's home number. Fourteen digits I will have to redial if my fingers go too fast in their excited haste. I sit in my garden so as not to disturb those in the house behind me, slumbering in its midnight hour, the time I have calculated will be best to find my friend at home considering the ten hour difference between our worlds.

Shrouded in darkness, I can still make out the dignified outlines of the cypresses standing guard over the garden I have grown to love. Behind them the Loquat tree spreads its arms wide, taking up space, finally at home among the mighty Oaks we found already planted when we arrived. It had taken nine long years to forgive me for pulling it out of my father's garden, housing it in a soda can, and carrying it on my lap on the plane ride across the world to this foreign soil. Nine years to send down roots and produce the sweet fruit of my childhood.

An owl's eerie screech reminds me of my mission and I check the time left until I make the birthday call. Twenty minutes to go before I can hear the crackle of thousands of miles between us, my voice flying over oceans and mountains, over deserts and cities, until it alights on Ronit's bedside table, where it rings her birthday awake.

"Aallo," I will hear her say, the emphasis leaning heavily on the first syllable of her greeting. Weariness and suspicion are always rolled into her tired voice, ready to do battle with an unwanted caller.

"Happy birthday old woman!" Only I can get away with this, reminding her that had she not been born a month prematurely, we would have shared the same birthday.

"Who are you calling old? You're next you know." And the voice I've carried in my heart all these years will have regained its lighter tone, its teasing and confiding lilt reserved for me. From there we will fill the space between us with brief accounts of events we missed in each other's lives, electrical signals transmitting our hopes and fears, our joys and sadness over the span of time and distance. This is the means by which we have learned the details of our separate lives; the birth of our children, the breakdown of her marriage, the start of a new one, the difficulty of her daily life with more duties now than dreams. We keep our calls short, all too aware of the cost of splurging on emotions, wishing for the simple pleasure of having a good laugh or cry over a cup of coffee in each other's kitchens. Every year this is our birthday gift to one another, a few moments of childhood voices echoing in our ears.

"Wish I were there to celebrate with you in person," I'll say like I do every year.

"Talk to you in exactly one month," she'll say, like she has for the past thirty years.

A rustling in the trees above me makes me remember why I'm giving up sleep tonight, and a glance through the window at the kitchen clock tells me it is time. I feel the familiar flutter of excitement in my stomach as I reach for the phone. Light from the kitchen falls on the page in the address book, and I start dialing the codes that connect us, arterial roads leading to the heart. One last number and my old friend will answer. A few moments of chatter will bring the smile back into her voice, and shake loose the accent that had been growing thicker in mine. But instead, the phone I'm gripping to my ear keeps ringing; its combination of long and short sound signals a Morse code of sorts. I let the ringing continue, tapping out its message, while I picture the inside of Ronit's house. Tile floors washed until they gleam, pink walls, still her favorite color, in the bathroom, every item neat and precisely in its place, my phone call the only jarring note in an otherwise orderly world. I look for her upstairs, where no one is allowed to bring food, her fear of roaches bordering on paranoia. I peek into the bomb shelter she has transformed into a pantry, into her daughters' rooms, their photographs replicas of their mother before the nose job. *Where are you?* But this is the first time my voice has not landed on its target, and I can picture it flailing through the air, skidding down the mountains, plunging into those oceans, losing the momentum that had propelled it from my darkened side of the world on the fifth of May to arrive on Ronit's sun-filled door step on the sixth.

By now the sky has darkened to a deeper shade of black, the moon hidden between the fan -like fronds of the palm trees that remind me of a distant landscape. I am certain there will be a logical explanation the next day, when I try to call again. But something has changed. A thin but precious thread broken as I push the off button on the now silent phone, and I'm left staring out into the immigrant garden I have created.

Two Sides

There are two ways of seeing the world, of being in the world. There are those of us who make our presence known, loudly demanding that we be heard, that our stories be told. Others fade into the background and let life simply happen to them, wash over them accepting what it brings. I can't seem to make up my mind, forever hovering between both. There are mornings when I wake up knowing that it's a red nail polish sort of day, a loud, I have something to declare kind of day. Those are dangerous times, when anything can happen, when the other side gets drowned out and I say what's in my heart. Those are walking in the rain without an umbrella kind of days, my face lifted towards the skies, the rain washing away all the uncertainty and yearning that made me have to be loud and paint my nails red in the first place. And then there are mornings when I wake up and feel the warmth emanating from the still sleeping form of my husband, and I know my place in the world and that everything will be all right.

Perhaps I can't make up my mind because the two sides aren't quite finished doing battle, accustomed to the schizophrenic dialogue of a life divided. Because I still recall waking up not knowing which side of the world I was on, whose room I was in, what time zone I inhabited, jetlag reminding me that I did not quite belong. I would listen for clues, the chatter of squirrels anchoring me in California, the call of a *muezzin* bringing me out of my sleep to the Middle East. I still catch myself wondering what my other world is doing, ten hours ahead and finished with the day I have just begun, as if they had had a head start on the book I've just started reading, and they'll know the ending before I do. Something is bound to be lost in translation, like the two versions of my family's past, each according to the parent being asked to remember. My father has chosen the darker rendition, leaving no room in his memory for lighthearted moments I know we must have had. Our house filled with sunshine and guests, the smell of fresh bread and sliced cucumbers, the feel of sun dried towels right off the line; And my mother gussying up for an outing, the scent of *Wind Song* perfume trailing behind her, the imprint of her lipstick kiss on the back of my hand, a rare gesture of warmth in the excitement of going out. Instead, my father conjures up tension and silence, arguing and drama, recalling my mother's harsh words on the way to the event then her forced smile as she outwardly admired him in public. A suffocating between walls where there were very clear wrongs and rights. I feel cheated by his version, as though my memories are merely figments of imagination, a misunderstanding of events because his truth was kept hidden from me.

My mother's version is brighter, as if my parents inhabited separate houses. Any challenge of her memories invites defensiveness and anger, a threat to the perfect family she insists we were, with her in the role of good wife and mother, we the dutiful children and misguided husband. "He's sick, she's brainwashed him. He will return," she claims and waits; years and youth slipping away. And I am left with a taste of both scripts, like the two languages I use interchangeably, my English strong and confident yet still peppered with Hebrew, while my Hebrew is strewn with English whenever I reach for a word and cannot find it.

For years I will struggle with these conflicting sides, convinced that I must choose one, declare my loyalties to the country, to the parent, to the correct rendering of the story. I will listen to my father's version, choose to keep him in my life, even find his new wife charming, a loyal friend in whom I learn to confide despite past betrayals. Then, within hours I am riddled with guilt, taking her deep interest and knowledge of my past as presumptuous rather than flattering, as if something has been taken away from me, a loss of self too willingly offered up.

Yet which self? Israeli or American? Loyal daughter to mother or father? Speaker of English with an accent no one can place, friend to those whom my mother detests? "I will never set foot in your house if you let that woman stay under your roof," my mother declares once I invite my father and Daniela back into our lives. Empty threats I have learned to ignore, no longer afraid. Which childhood did I have, the one my father tries to forget, or the one my mother preserves, our history touted while she refuses to see the truth, a child closing one eye and making half the world disappear. Even my parents' depiction of me as a child rings different, depending on the narrator. Pride in her voice, my mother recalls what a "good girl" I was, always singing, so well-mannered, sitting quietly like a little lady through an entire opera she smuggled me into at age three. My father summons a different version of an obedient, fearful little girl, unsmiling and sad. And what does it matter? Both sides are part of this self that surely must have formed by now. I have been between places for too long. It is time to land.

Taste Test

Israel, 2002

I make up for time away from my country by eating my way through it when I return. Before the plane's wheels touch Israeli soil I can already taste the bottled juice my father will have prepared for the long drive to his house. Apricot and peach nectar, sweet and thick, a welcome change from the American ginger ale I sipped on my way across the oceans. I taste America as well, but the flavors are fleeting, contrived, fizz and pop, new and improved. It is the old and familiar that I seek when I return. For my first evening back, his joy at finding me seated at his kitchen table still in his eyes, my father surprises me with a childhood memory. Out of the refrigerator where he's kept it chilled, he produces *Sabres*, the fruit of the prickly pear, peeled of its thorns, its sweet heart waiting for me. I am delighted. Not just because my first bite into its juicy flesh fills my mouth with summer days at the beach where he once bought me this cool treat. But more so because the man who always seemed as if he existed in the family's margins, had been paying attention all along and had stored this bit of information about me.

Next morning at the beach, I know exactly what the bikini clad waitress will bring when I ask for a plate of fries, once I remember that they are called chips on that side of the world. Each one thick and golden nestled next to a generous dollop of hummus and warm pita bread. If I'm too impatient I will burn my tongue. If I wait too long the sea breeze will have cooled my meal. My American husband soon becomes a fan of this early ocean-side repast, and our children will forever associate beach visits with the warm smell of fries.

Back in the city, on the street corner where I used to break into a run in case the bus was already waiting at its stop, still stands a large cauldron, corn on the cob rolling in the boiling water. Sweet vapors rise and mingle with the bus fumes, following me as I board and take my seat. From the window my view includes the *Shuarma* stand, the Middle East's version of fast food. Skewered lamb meat is slowly turning on a spit, tantalizing to the passersby who can smell it roasting a block away. I keep my seat despite the great temptation.

In just a few hours, while the cities still sleep under their blankets of stars, bakers will rise to start ovens that will soon produce loaves of dark bread I was sent to buy as a child. The early morning air seemed filled with the crisp crust smell, the bread thickly sliced and offered on the breakfast table with my father's homemade jam. The jam jars could be filled with anything he saw fit to preserve; Mulberries, apricots or loquats from his trees. And one year green tomatoes I was brave enough to taste and which he faithfully plowed through, not wanting to waste, despite the questionable flavor. Back in America, I will once again stand in the bread aisle, marveling before the twenty-three types of bread from which I may choose. I know because I counted them one day. I will learn to make PB and J's, learn to handle the snow white bread my children will demand for their grilled cheese sandwiches, a culinary art form my American husband will share with me. And no one will understand why I linger by the specialty breads at the local grocery, those simple earthy loaves conjuring up my childhood.

Even my visit to the outdoor market under old *Acco's* street level, helps me on my edible tour through old haunts. The air is thicker here, redolent with a mixture only a returning native can appreciate. Once the eyes become accustomed to the dimness broken only by occasional gaps in the awnings above; the many sources of the smells become visible to the eye. Long tables stretch into the narrow passageway, freshly caught fish displayed on beds of ice, dripping onto the cobbled walk below. I tuck my toes into my sandals as I breathe in the scent of sea air wafting from the shiny scales. Mangy cats, their eyes hungry, have placed themselves strategically under these tables, hoping for more than the fishy puddles collecting between the stones. Further down the alley an Arab woman is flattening pita dough against a pillow that has seen better days, and the smell of *Zataar* sprinkled over the baked flat bread impels me to purchase another taste of my past, coating my fingers and lips in the fragrant olive oil to which the spice adheres. A small shop, from a distance no more than a dent in the wall, draws me in to its cavern-like depths. Burlap sacks filled with spices and beans line the cement floor. The scent of coffee mingles with the perfumed smell of cardamom, sweet cinnamon, raw sugar. Rock candy glistens from a corner, like rough diamonds waiting to be plucked from the earth, while my hand trails in a sack of velvety lentils, the shop's owner wondering at my joy over the simplicities of his life. He offers a small cup of Turkish coffee, a hospitable gesture I reciprocate by leaving his store with small packets of several items for my return to America. Once there I will measure out these treasures, store them in small glass jars and uncork them to inhale the comforting scents of my past whenever I want to visit.

I want to taste everything, take it all back with me to the land where I have chosen to make my home, even though my senses hunger for the flavors of another world, another time. These foods with which I fill myself carry within them a part of me, of every season I have spent in this faraway place. They call to me, whispering reminders of a lifetime ago. Large, soft pretzels we always bought on our trips to Jerusalem covered in sesame seeds we'd find hours later, stowaways in the folds of our clothes. Fragile chocolate domes, wrapped in silvery foil, their centers filled with a snowy white crème and sold only in the winter. And Guavas. Long before I recognize their smooth skins beckoning me from the vendor's bin, their summery scent sings to me of orchards an old uncle once owned, his crumbling stone house dipped in the shadow of leafy branches and the dizzying perfume of the fruit's ripeness. My mouth remembers their taste, like recognizing an old friend's voice, while my tongue feels the tiny seeds I must avoid before they embed themselves in my teeth.

Tonight, as I pack our suitcases for the return flight to California, I fill with the flavors of my past all the spaces emptied of gifts I had brought for friends. There between the summer shirts I tuck three bags of Turkish coffee; just enough if we save its thick sweet smell for leisurely enjoyment on weekends. Lining the bottom of the case are two bags of pita bread. Plump and soft, nothing like the ones sold at the local Safeway, despite the authentic desert scene imprinted on the made in America package. The last of the space is taken up by tins of green olives, fruit of the gnarled trees that dot the hills of a landscape the briny flavor will evoke. Our luggage is zipped, tagged, brought to the front door through which we will leave before the next morning has had a chance to shake itself of its dreams. The cases are heavy as is my heart at yet another goodbye. But the heart is also filled, my hunger for this land temporarily sated until I may eat at its tables again.

Releasing Ghosts

Israel, Evening, July 10, 2006

The night before we leave for America, father gives us a going away party in the garden that is not his garden. And his wife, who is not my mother, welcomes pieces of a past that is not hers to share. My third grade teacher arrives, and spends the evening sitting with my nine-year old daughter doing what she knows best, teaching. An old classmate holds my hands and stares. "You haven't changed a bit," she says. And neither has she, except for the high heels which make her tower over me, and the fancy makeup behind which I can still see the girl in pigtails that used to sit in class and click her gum behind me. An old uncle holds my face between his hands. "You have Irka's eyes," he states, seeing my dead grandmother's face in mine. There are ghosts everywhere. But it is time to quiet their voices. Time to choose the language in which I can bid them farewell, set them loose between these pages until someone else may want to visit them so they and I can rest.

Going Home

Israel, Morning, July 11, 2006

The airport official is young, her hair as curly as mine only darker, no gray snaking through it yet. The sun has barely had time to warm the day, and her face already shows all the signs of boredom and weariness. I smile warmly, a habit I have adopted from my American husband, a way to charm even the most disgruntled government employee. "Good morning!" I announce in my heaviest American accent, offering a fistful of American passports through the narrow opening in her glass cage. She eyes me suspiciously, mistrusting my early morning cheerfulness, thumbs through the paperwork, and stops so abruptly that I know she must have arrived at mine. I have been caught again, trying not to be me.

"Your identity number," she commands, weariness gone from her tone. Now she is awake.

"What do you mean?" I ask innocently, still trying and rapidly failing to keep the *Sabra* tucked out of view, the daggers out of my eyes, the edge out of my voice, the anger I know is on its way out of the slight shaking in my knees. And I am seeing myself repeating a scene which has become a familiar dance between two countries, both claiming me as their own, yet one does so more aggressively, threateningly, not accustomed to losing her battles.

"Your identity number is in your Israeli passport" the clerk explains, impatience creeping into her voice, her eyes holding mine as if to say she's giving me one last chance.

"I don't have one," I lie, my expired Israeli passport pulsing

| 219

slightly in my purse, trying to give me away. I clasp the bag a little closer to my side, as if the document inside could wiggle its way out and expose me, ruin the decision I had already made on the train ride to the airport. The clerk eyes me, contempt in her gaze, and turns to the phone hanging on the wall of her cubicle. I hold her eyes with mine as she switches to Hebrew and summons re- inforcements for the problem standing before her. I dare a glance at my husband whose eyes are rolling at what he knows is sure to come. And as if on cue, a tall woman is rushing towards me, determination stamped on her tight-lipped face.

"Your identity number!" she practically yells in my face, as I straighten myself for some extra height.

"I still don't have one," I hiss back, "and you don't have to yell," I add, ignoring my husband's attempt to catch my attention and my children's wide-eyed stares.

"I'm not yelling," she yells. "But if you want to leave today I need your Israeli passport!"

I am just now beginning to notice the crowd behind us, star- ing intently at this early morning drama unfolding before them. The threat of detaining me has done away with my last attempt at polite American control, the thought of that plane leaving without me unbearable.

"I'm an American citizen and I don't live here," I declare. "I haven't lived here for over twenty years, and if you threaten me I won't be coming back!" I want to go home, the thought hitting me with clarity it has never had before.

"With this kind of behavior we don't WANT you here!" She retorts, and the hand I plunge into my purse has figured out what it has to do even before I have a chance to think this through, as I pull out the Israeli passport and throw it at the angry stranger in front of me.

"Take it. Keep it. I won't be needing it anymore." I have

switched to Hebrew without even noticing, measuring out my words carefully so their meaning will not be lost on either one of us. I don't want to make a mistake in the language in which I no longer live, taking the official and myself by surprise as she stomps away with my claim to citizenship in her hand. I refuse to meet my husband's eyes, knowing all too well the disappointment I would see reflected there; The words that would be sure to follow if I gave him a chance to say them, which I don't. But I can hear them anyway as I stand facing the clerk whose eyes look almost regretful for the mess she could have avoided. *You're such an Israeli*, my American husband is silently saying to my back, his favorite insult when I have misbehaved and slipped into my former self, the one I took so long to wake and don't really want to shove back into the genie's bottle. The one I allowed out in my father's garden the night before, when the sadness of the next day's goodbyes spilled out using all the wrong words and turning into anger he translated as weakness. Anger he no longer needed once he had found his place in the world. But I was still searching, for the land that would feel like home, for the people who would remember what had been before it all changed, for the voice in which to say it all. And anger seemed to keep the tears at bay, and I could not afford tears right now.

The official has returned, our documents in hand, and without a word she offers them back, my Israeli passport included just in case I change my mind. We're free to leave and I stride ahead, not looking back but trusting that my husband and children are in tow. The faster I walk the less chance that they will see the tears that are now coming hot and furious. I make my way to the gate where a tall man is wrapped and swaying in his prayer shawl. From a far corner cigarette smoke is pouring out of the smoking section where the door has been propped open for air by the very same people polluting it. "Idiots," I mutter as

I throw myself into an empty seat, although I'm also grateful for the added cause for anger, which makes leaving that much easier. My husband and children have been following at a safe distance, he placing a hot cup of coffee in my hands, while they glue themselves to the large window to watch the planes. The coffee helps, warm liquid washing away tension that had been gathering for the last three weeks, even when I didn't know it. I thought I could do it, face old friends, old haunts, introduce the present to the past, not realizing that the past was present in every turn. Not just when I chose to bring the two together. Despite my acceptance of Daniela, my good sense telling me that she made my father happy which he finally deserved to be, the little girl in me still found it difficult to see him as someone else's husband, father to another man's children. That past was in the handful of items I recognized on my father's shelves, a statue here, a vase there, bits and pieces from a past life taking me by surprise in new surroundings. The past was in the voice of my grandmother's oldest friend, even before she opened the door to let us in. "Karushka!" Her endearing name for me a sound I had almost forgotten. Still sharp, no nonsense like all the women her age who suffered more than any human should. I had to escape into her tiny kitchen when the phone rang and she switched to Polish. It was as if no time had passed and she could very well have been talking to my dead grandmother. Even the kitchen offered little refuge, everything about it reminding me of other kitchens. Old dish towels worn to bare threads, pots predating the war that brought their owners to this land. Everything saved by women who knew what not having meant. All these reminders were too sad, not because of what they represented, but because I had never been given the choice of saying goodbye, never allowed to decide what I wanted to be. Was I the Californian returning to her native land? The Israeli exile pretending to be

American? A tourist bearing gifts for old friends, returning with Middle Eastern souvenirs to hang on her American walls?

And now, minutes before boarding would be announced, the tail ends of my anger evaporating around the corner of the terminal, I finally thought I knew. There would always be a place for me on this side of the world. A bed made in my father's new house. A plate filled at my best friend's table; People who would include me in their thoughts and hearts, missing me when I was gone. But I had become more visitor than resident, my camera at the ready to capture images I no longer assumed I'd see again. I now relied on photographs, on notes carefully recorded in a journal packed for the occasion. These tools would help me stop time, preserve it before people moved and strangers' faces looked out of familiar windows. Before loved ones died and their images danced away, and buildings in which I'd spent my childhood were torn down. Before change came and I'd forget while becoming someone else, joining that life I was waiting to begin while it had kept going without me. The balance had shifted, and when the plane touched down in San Francisco, the airport official checking my passport would welcome me home, and I'd be there.

In the Morning Hours

California, July 12, 2006, 2:01 p.m.

(Israel, July 13, 12:01, a.m.)

Katyusha rockets hit Haifa's crowded industrial zone in the morning hours. One of the rockets directly hit an Israel Railways train depot, killing eight workers.

A woman was killed by a rocket in the morning hours of the war's second day. The Nahariya hospital filled up with injured people, both residents and soldiers.

The phone is ringing, as if whoever is on the other end knows we have returned and can't be made to wait until we've settled in. I stand in the familiar surroundings of my room, longingly eyeing the bed I'd missed after three weeks of someone else's mattress under my back, and nearly twenty-four hours of sitting in cramped plane seats and airport terminals. I can hear the children's happy voices down the hall, greeting toys they'd missed, the dog's giddy barking at finding his owners restored. Back to normal, I think as I reach for the phone, my sweater still hanging over my arm as I sink into the comfort of my favorite armchair. "Hello?"

"Allo, it's me, are you okay?" Ronit's voice takes me by surprise. I'd seen her less than forty-eight hours ago, not enough time for her to have missed me.

"Ronit! We just walked in. Miss me already?" I wait for her laugh but it doesn't come, and the silence makes me sit up from my slumped position.

"The war started. Lebanon attacked, right after you left. The train you took to the airport was bombed." Her voice is hushed, as if saying this out loud will make it more frightening than it already is.

"Where are you? Are you all right?" I stare out into the garden I had been eager to tend, aware of all the weeding and cleaning awaiting me after three weeks of neglect. All I can picture though is the inside of Ronit's house, how close it is to the Lebanese border, the direction from which the attack is coming.

"We're in the bomb shelter. I can hear the rockets falling and the girls are hysterical." I strain to hear the war outside her walls, the very same walls I stood between just a hand-full of hours ago when she had given us a tour of her home. This shelter was nothing like the community shelter we had grown up with as girls, dirty and dusty and filled with anxious neighbors. This was a privately owned strong room she used as a pantry when war wasn't raging outside her window. I had admired her laden shelves, supplies of olives, rice, jams, and chocolate, carefully arranged in neat rows.

"You've been in there since we left?" While I flew away from her once again, her night turning into my day, I was retreating from danger, and she was in its midst.

"The girls and I are sleeping on mattresses, and we're only leaving the room when we have to since the rockets are too close."

"Where's Eitan?" I could imagine the already strained marriage pushed to its limits in such confined space for that many hours.

"Eitan was called to his unit, and the girls and I will go to relatives in Tel Aviv when the roads are opened again." Everything had shut down, cars abandoned where their drivers had come to a screeching halt. Apartments were left unlocked, dinners abandoned on tables as residents fled to shelters at the siren's warning wail. The coastal town of Nahariya had turned into a ghost town, its tourists confined to their hotels, restaurants emptied, night-clubs silenced, and there was nothing I could do to save my friend.

"Ronit…" I don't know what to say, a helplessness weighing me down at the thought of anything happening to this piece of my heart I left behind. She had stood in the doorway of my father's house as other guests were saying goodbye the night of our farewell party. I hadn't been ready for her to leave, my mind still searching for anything I may have forgotten to tell her about the last five years when I was away. But her husband had been impatient, sending dark looks I could see and she could sense as she sat facing me, her back absorbing his mounting unrest. I wanted to sit with her on the edge of my bed the way we did when we were girls, and see her face explode into laughter, or her eyes widen in amazement as I told her about my life in America. Instead, our eyes locked over the heads of departing guests, and before I could stop her, she had raised her right hand in a hurried wave and turned her back to run up the garden steps to the road above, out of my sight. Despite years of practice she was still no good at goodbyes.

"You get out of there the minute you can, you hear? Get on a plane and come here if you want. I mean it." Ronit had never been to America, not yet seen the place I now called home. This seemed like as good a time as any to introduce her to my side of the world where nothing but soft rain, or the lonely whistle of a train disturbed the early morning hours.

"I'd love to come, but even if we could afford it, there wouldn't be any seats left at this point. Everyone's heading for the airport." She would have to wait this one out until the shelling stopped ten days later, and the smoke-filled streets of the quaint sea-side town were cleared of debris. And I would have to accept the fact that our lives were very different now, each of us having made choices that would fill our morning hours with very different sounds.

Arriving

California, 2007

Somehow when I wasn't watching my heart must have loosened the strings that bound it to the land I once called home. And just like that, I was free. This new love had come quietly, without fanfare. It wasn't love at first sight, fireworks; bells and whistles. This was calmer, steady, a deep friendship with a place now familiar and dear. I knew I had arrived when I heard my son's laughter in the next room. When I looked out the kitchen window and saw my daughter perched between the branches of the Ginkgo tree, my own personal garden fairy. When the crocuses remembered to emerge last spring, and the apples fattened on the tree we planted. When the hummingbirds chose *our* garden to hover and alight, stilling their wings in a rare moment of respite; when dear friends gave up their Saturday to cut down a tree broken by a winter storm.

I hadn't noticed that the life I was waiting to begin had been forming all around me; wrapping me in its vines and making me part of the tapestry. While I had travelled the world searching, what I was looking for was on my doorstep all along. I knew that the loud squawking came from bluebirds announcing the morning before I was ready to greet it. The dog would be in my bed if I didn't get up fast enough. The oranges suspended from their branches would ripen and appear in our bedroom window as if framed in a winter scene. The click of metal at the end of the day would be my husband folding his glasses and settling into sleep. Background music for whatever dream enveloped me would be the shrill, haunting whistle of the two a.m. train on its way through town.

It had arrived, the calm and confidence for which I always yearned. The voice hiding inside me all along, the one that had been drowned out by the loudness of fear and doubt, could now say its piece. The heart, closed against hurt, was opened to love I no longer worried would disappear.

And once a year, the white haired man sitting in my garden, a book in one hand and a grandchild on his lap would be my father, enjoying the fruits of a garden he planted so long ago. I had found my place in the world.

Author, age 2, with father, in Michigan

Author with Janek, maternal step-grandfather, Jerusalem, Israel 1966

Author age 2, waiting for favorite ride in grandmother's VW

Author learning to read Hebrew with her father, California, 1971

Fifth grade class, Israel 1977, author seated fourth from left.

Paul Kelen, author's paternal step-grandfather

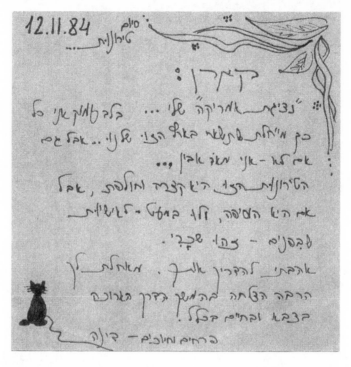

Note from bootcamp officer, November 12, 1984, Israel

End of bootcamp...
Karen: My "American representative"... with a deep heart I so wish that you will stay in this country of ours... yet even if not—I will so understand... Bootcamp is short and fleeting, yet if it added, and even a little, to the personality inside—that is my pay. I loved leading you. Wishing you much success in the continued and lengthy journey in the military and in life in general.

Flowers and smiles
—Dinna

Author during bootcamp, Israel 1984

Wedding day, Israel 1993

Ronit, Author and Lee reunited, Israel 2000

Author and husband, Mark, Israel 1993

Author's father in California garden with grandchildren, Bailey and Emma

HOMEBOUND
PUBLICATIONS

AT HOMEBOUND PUBLICATIONS WE RECOGNIZE THE IM-
PORTANCE of going home to gather from the stores of old
wisdom to help nourish our lives in this modern era. We
choose to lend voice to those individuals who endeavor to
translate the old truths into new context and keep alive
through the written word ways of life that are now endan-
gered. Our titles introduce insights concerning mankind's
present internal, social and ecological dilemmas.

It is our intention at Homebound Publications to
revive contemplative storytelling. We publish full-length
introspective works of: non-fiction, essay collections, epic
verse, short story collections, journals, travel writing, and
novels. In our fiction titles our intention is to introduce
new perspectives that will directly aid mankind in the trials
we face at present.

It is our belief that the stories humanity lives by give
both context and perspective to our lives. Some older stories, while well-known to the generations, no longer reso-
nate with the heart of the modern man nor do they address
the present situation we face individually and as a global
village. Homebound chooses titles that balance a reverence
for the old sensibilities; while at the same time presenting
new perspectives by which to live.

CPSIA information can be obtained
at www.ICGtesting.com
Printed in the USA
FSOW02n2221190915
11180FS